# Annoyed With Lloyd

B.E.N.T.
Biological Enhanced Nascent Talent

## By Christopher Woods

Three Ravens Publishing
Chickamauga, GA USA

This one is dedicated to David and Candi Webb.

We spent hours and hours umpteen years ago drawing pictures and reading my stories aloud. They were there when Alex Lloyd was brought into this world.

Love you guys!

Chris

# Chapter 1

"…Japanese Emperor Hijiro is due to arrive in Los Angeles this morning to start his first American tour…"

I sighed. Most days I tried to forget about the B.E.N.T. but it's hard to do when one of the strongest of us is tromping through the country. Biologically enhanced nascent talent. That's what the powers that be had decided to call those of us who'd been affected after the fifties. 1954, another thing I didn't like to think about.

"Any chance you can turn that station?" I asked the tall blond behind the bar. She was a little over six feet tall and built like a model. The only issue for most people would be the beard.

"That's gonna be on every station, honey." She kept wiping at the mess on the end of the bar. "I can change it, but they'll all be the same."

"Shit," I muttered.

She turned to me and shrugged with the long beard resting between her breasts. Seeing where I was looking, she chuckled.

"I tried cutting the damn thing," she said. "It grows back in about three hours. It stops when it hits this length."

I sighed again.

She snorted. "Ridiculous Bend, don't you think?"

"Met a guy in Dallas who had hair about that length all over."

"That has to be a pain," she said. "Most days I can flip this thing back over my shoulder and feel almost like a normal woman."

"Ain't no fun in bein' normal, darlin'. Most of the norms are just boring as hell."

"Sounds like a BENT thing to say." She cocked her head to the side a fraction. "What's your Bend?"

I looked around at the empty bar and laid my hand on the counter, then concentrated. It seemed to melt as it flattened across the bar top.

"Holy shit! A shapeshifter? You're a Talent."

"Yeah," I said as I glanced at the television again where the Emperor's ship had just eased into the port. "Nothing like that guy, though."

"Not many people can do anything like him," she said as she looked at the screen. "Most people these days haven't even seen what he could do. Just what we've seen in the history vids. What he did to China in '56 was recorded."

"The vids they show today only cover about half of it. It was a live broadcast back then. Before they scrubbed a lot of the devastation. This whole tour is some sort of rebranding effort for the guy. We're lucky he stopped with the Far East and didn't decide to pick back up the mantle of world conqueror. I guess taking China and all the smaller countries was enough for him."

"You sound like you were there," she said. "You're not that old."

I reformed the hand I had laid on the bar. "Shapeshifter. I don't usually look my age."

"Ah, I see."

"I'm about to close up shop," she said. "You're the last one here. Do you mind if I go ahead and lock up? No rush for you to leave but I can start cleaning up."

"No problem." I grinned as she bent down to pick something from the floor.

She looked back and caught me.

Standing back up, she turned back toward me. "So, what would you think about coming upstairs and I'll shave this thing off where we can have a little fun?"

I grinned. "No need to go to all that trouble. Leave it be. I told you norms are boring."

She smiled.

I ordered a cup of coffee and spent the next thirty minutes watching her clean around the bar room. The TV was still spouting off about the Japanese Emperor and how he was doing his goodwill tour of the world.

"Need some good will after the shit you've done," I muttered at the screen.

I was relieved when she returned and cut the TV off. A few minutes later, I followed her through the door to the stairs.

"So, what other parts can you shift?"

I chuckled. "All the parts, darlin'."

"Oh, my…"

The sun was bright as I stepped out of Lillana's Waypoint. I remembered when smog was so thick in LA you could cut it with a knife. Then Brandlewine showed up on her quest to save the planet. Her Bend fed on most of the elements that made up the heavy clouds around the place. She spent weeks absorbing it and flew off into the distance. LA was a lot nicer after that.

I had no doubts it would build up again with all the traffic that ran the roads. But for a while, there was a pleasant blue sky above.

According to the news, she was in London now.

"Good luck there, Brandy," I said.

I slipped into the alley beside Lillana's and closed my eyes for a moment. Small shifts crawled around my body, and I opened green eyes instead of brown. I was six inches shorter, a bit stouter, and sported a long red beard. My clothes didn't fit right anymore but I was only a half block from a Hallmart. It didn't cost overly much to buy a few clothes.

I only had to do this when I got too close to anyone. Lillana had been nice. Sometimes I let down my guard and let something slip. I wasn't sure if I had this time, but it was possible. If the authorities found me, it would probably get ugly. They still had me on the most wanted list in every one of the three-letter organizations.

In their defense, I killed a lot of people in '58. They killed my brother and they died for it. It was a dark time for me.

I paid for my clothes after a short shopping spree and took them to the bathroom where I changed. Nothing fancy, just something simple and inconspicuous. Just blue jeans, a flannel shirt, and work boots. I'd seen a Goodwill bin outside, so I dropped the old clothes into the bin on my way out the door. They were nice quality clothes since I'd been an "executive" before I changed. It really was a nice suit, and I was going to miss it.

The current visage would serve me better where I was heading. All I needed was to go to Kelen's place and pick up a new ID. I tried to avoid the whole body changes so I could use the ID without replacing it. But it was time to go east. I was tired of LA and had a little business to take care of in New York. I would need the new persona for that.

I sat down on the bench for the nearest bus stop and waited, watching the people as they walked by. A couple strolled at a leisurely pace hand in hand. They were giggling and pointing in different directions.

"Tourists," I mumbled.

Both of them stopped as a large digital sign showed Emperor Hijiro walking down an elaborate walkway from his ship.

I shook my head. They were both young enough to think he was some sort of hero after uniting the Far East. He'd personally killed more people than cancer. I guess a few million people were a drop in the bucket to the billions of citizens of the Empire. I still remembered the Tsunami that hit southern China. Millions died after "Jishin" ruptured a fault line and caused an earthquake under the Pacific.

"It's Quake," the young man said.

In 1956 they'd tried to shoot him, but he was bulletproof. They bombed him but he walked out of the crater pissed as hell and made the earth swallow Beijing. It took a lot of killing to take China, but he did it. He bought his empire with blood, a lot of it innocent.

But they don't teach that in schools anymore. Hijiro's body count dwarfed even the Nazis of World War Two. I wondered how that would have gone if the asteroid had come fifteen years earlier than it had. If it had come in '39 instead of '54 I had a feeling WW2 would have been a lot bloodier than it already was.

Sometimes I just had to shake my head as people like these two kids cheered a mass-murdering dictator.

"They just don't know any better," I said.

The bus pulled up at the stop and I climbed the steps to take a seat at the back. I preferred not to have my back exposed. I'm not sure why I bothered. My particular Bend would let me heal any injury almost instantaneously. Although, these days, I'd found that I had to concentrate harder to do what I used to do without much thought. Now there was a much more noticeable limit to what I could do.

I guess my age was telling a little. I'd be turning ninety-three this year, so I couldn't complain too much.

# Chapter 2

Kelen's place wasn't in an obvious location. It never was. Kelen liked to move around, and he'd only let certain people know when he moved. He'd been in LA for a few years now and I stopped by every so often just to check-in. It had been close to a year since my last visit though. I entered the hair salon and glanced around.

"Oh, honey… you have come to the right place." The hairdresser was shaking a finger at me. He wore a tight white shirt with yellow pants and held one of those fancy cigarette holders in his other hand. "*You* need some help." He looked at me like he was sizing up a hunk of meat.

I grinned. "So, a nun walks into a bar…"

Kelen let out a long sigh with the finger still wagging at me. "Fuck. Now I *know* you didn't do that to yourself on purpose. Even *you* have a little more style than this, Alexander Lloyd."

I looked around at the use of my name.

"Oh, hush, sweetie. You know my place is safe." Kelen looked around. "Or did you bring some with you again?"

"That only happened the *one* time," I said.

"And destroyed my venerable establishment."

"It was a whore house, Kel."

"It was a damned venerable whore house."

I chuckled. "How the hell are ya?"

"I was doing lovely until this Irish dwarf walked through my door." He waved his hand around motioning toward me. "What can I do for America's most wanted, today? Is anyone coming in behind you with guns, knives, or…tanks?"

"Worse case, there might be a gorgeous blonde with a beard."

Kelen stopped and looked at me with one eyebrow raised. "I don't think I even want to know."

"Probably not."

He sighed. "Follow me." He glanced up and down my body and shook his head. "Fucking leprechaun."

I chuckled again and followed him into the back where one of his staff was sweeping. She looked to be about five and a half feet tall with jet-black hair.

Kelen glanced at me and coughed. "Don't get any ideas. She doesn't like your type."

"That hurts Kel. You know I can be any type, right?"

"She don't mess with the BENT."

The girl was staring at me with ice-blue eyes.

"Shame," I said with a grin.

"Go watch the front for me, Bets," Kelen said. "I have to do some work in the back."

Bets nodded and walked toward the front. She gave me a crooked grin as she passed. I figured she was hit on fairly regularly by every straight guy who came in.

**Half the women, too**.

I stopped in my tracks. "What the fuck?" The voice had been in my head.

"Oh, girl! What *are* you thinking?"

"He's not saying anything. He's even more wanted than I am."

"Just go to the front, girl." He motioned toward me. "*You* come with me and keep your cake hole shut."

"But—"

"You heard me."

I followed Kelen into a hidden door and down a set of stairs wondering why the hell he had a telepath working the salon. And *how* the hell did he have a telepath at all?

"Go ahead and ask."

"You know what they'll do if they find her."

"That's why it's my job to see to it they don't," he said. "Stupid things like that make it more difficult."

"She heard you say my name. I'm probably one of the safest people to do that with."

"True, but it was still stupid." He looked toward the ceiling. "I know you hear me, girl."

"Gotta be hard keeping something like that secret," I said. "It's necessary, but hard."

"As you well know," he said.

For a moment I saw Adam laying in my arms gasping for breath. His last words echoed in my mind for years. He'd never spoken them, but I heard them.

**I'm sorry.**

He'd sent those words to me because his lungs were filled with blood from the bullets. I lost my brother that day. They lost a lot more afterward.

I shook my head and followed Kelen to a small computer station that looked like it came from the '80s.

"Still using that?"

"Honey, you know it's not the computer that does all this, don't you?"

"Yeah, it just seems like you would upgrade to something a little more modern."

"Oh sweetie, I'm as modern as it gets. What does my Irish dwarf need?"

"Actually, I need about four different deep backgrounds and a few surface ones. The Irish dwarf only needs to be shallow. I'll shift for the pictures if you have some other clothes and stuff."

"You must have a large job lined up."

"Pretty big."

"Who's going to lose a fortune in the near future?"

"You heard of the Kazaskis in New York?"

"That's a big target, are you sure? I thought you stayed out of New York."

"Normally I would. The Kazaskis are huge in the drug trade and gambling. I can respect that. But lately, they've been dealing with some Romanians and some human trafficking. You know how I feel about that."

"I do."

"They took a particular girl and I've been hired to get her back. If I can, I will. If I can't, I'm burning it down."

"You don't deal in half measures."

I smiled.

"Have a seat over there. This is gonna take a little while. I'll have some pictures soon to match and we'll get current updates of them when you do your thing. Right now, I'll do my thing."

He placed his hand on the ancient pc and the hair stood up on my arms as he began to glow. Then he seemed to break down into single particles flowing into the computer and was gone.

"That's weird every time," I muttered, looking at the pile of clothes that fell to the floor.

# Chapter 3

"These will do nicely," I said as I pulled a dress and a tuxedo from the rack.

"She's pretty," Kelen said.

"She's bait."

"I can see that working, sweetie, but you need something besides that dress to use for the picture. People don't wear fine clothes like that to the DMV."

"These are for the job. I gotta have a wardrobe for seven people."

"I was afraid you were going to say that when you took down that Armani. You *do* know that's a three thousand dollar tux, don't you?"

I poked my finger through the small hole in the back of the jacket.

He grinned. "Well… it *was* a three thousand dollar tux."

I chuckled. "I can patch it."

"What? Are you a seamstress now?"

"You learn a few things if you live long enough. It should be relatively unnoticeable."

"I'll give you a discount since the hole goes through the shirt too."

I chuckled again. "Looks like a certain stiletto."

"Some people think they can do whatever they want because they have money. This one found out that he was incorrect."

"I'm guessing he deserved it. You don't go around killin' folks all willy-nilly like that guy in Frisco. What was his name?"

"Yarborough, the Transformer."

"Yeah, that guy. Talent like that could have been really useful to the world. Hell, he could have made a fortune as a plastic surgeon." I laid the dress and tux on a table.

"He could transform anyone except himself. Used it to kill eighty-three women before someone managed to stab him eighty-three times. No one knows who it was that rid the world of that asshole."

"You did the world a favor, Kel."

"I never said—"

"You didn't have to. I was there. You beat me to it."

"You never said anything."

"I knew the guy had it coming. I was there to do it myself, but you handled it nicely. Sadly, you couldn't take the time to make him suffer for what he did to those women."

"Too dangerous to live." Pausing, he frowned. "The same thing the CIA goons said about telepaths, isn't it?"

"Yeah, but we'd seen what he was doing. Government snatched the telepaths even when they didn't do anything."

"That's why I didn't tell you. I thought you would think I was as bad as them."

"You're worlds better than they were." I placed a delicate hand on his shoulder.

"You know it's really freaky when you're half knockout gorgeous and the other half leprechaun, right?"

"You have no idea how freaky it can get."

Kelen shook his head. "I'm fairly certain I do *not* want to know."

"Turned into a goat-headed demon halfway through the act while I was with this chick that was a Satanist. Scared her so bad she's an Evangelical preacher on TV now."

"That's vaguely familiar... oh my god, are you talking about...?"

"Yep."

"Evangeline? The one with the angel wings?"

"She wasn't quite as pure when she was in her twenties. Had this cult starting up in Philadelphia. I wondered how far she ran until I saw her on TV one day preaching about forgiveness."

"She has a sermon about that night. I thought it was a metaphor." Kelen laughed. "I had no idea."

"I don't usually talk about it." I paused. "I don't think I ever told anyone about that before."

"Who do you have to talk to that wouldn't turn you in for the bounty?"

"True enough. I haven't figured out why you didn't turn me in a long time ago."

"Then I wouldn't hear how the Angel of Rox Network got her start and other tales that I'll add to the book I plan to write."

"Don't go exaggerating things, now."

"Hmpf." He chuckled. "Like I have to exaggerate."

I laughed as I slid into the red dress. "In all seriousness, though, you have to get that girl out of here. She's young enough not to have seen what they did to her kind. What they'll *do* to her. I'm not even sure the BRM could protect her."

The BENT Rights Movement was pretty active in the US, but I wasn't sure they could match the CIA.

"I try to tell her, but I don't think she believes me."

"She needs to see it, Kel. Call her down here. I can show her first-hand what they do to telepaths."

Annoyed with Lloyd

# Chapter 4

May 23, 1954: Topeka, Kansas

"Here's to the end of the world," Adam said as he raised his beer toward me.

I stretched, reaching over with mine and tapped the bottles together. "The end of the world!"

We drank deeply and watched the sky.

"What do you think it'll do?" I asked.

"They say it's bigger than the one that wiped out the dinosaurs. I expect it'll be fairly quick. The scientists say it'll impact somewhere over the Midwest."

"To think," I said. "We survived the biggest war the planet has ever seen only to be squashed by a big rock from space."

"I know. It's not cool at all."

"They say we have about thirty minutes before we'll see it in the sky," I said. "At least we're at ground zero. We'll see the show close up."

"Well, drink up little brother," he said with his beer held toward the sky. "Sure don't want to be sober for this."

I took a long drink, emptying my fourth beer. "I should have picked up some rum. That's what happens when I let you get the drinks. We end up with beer."

"Don't have time to make it to the store for rum, now. You're just going to have to make the best of it."

"Look!" I pointed into the sky where I could see the shape forming. "I can see it in the middle of the day!"

"That's insane," Adam gasped. "But it's coming right at us, so it stands to reason we would be able to see it as it gets closer. They say when it hits the atmosphere it will start to burn."

I looked at him as he stared into the sky. "I love you brother."

He nodded and turned to me. "Love you too kid."

We both looked up as the sky turned blood red. The rock had flamed alright, but something happened. We stood staring into the sky, waiting for the end that didn't come.

"What happened?" I asked as the red sky grew above us. Soon it stretched all the way to the horizon.

"Well, shit." He looked over at me. "Maybe I should have gone to work after all. Seems like the end is going to have to wait awhile."

There seemed to be a red haze forming in the sky.

"Did it just dissolve?" I asked.

"I guess it did," he said as the red haze dropped around us like a cloud of fine dust.

I reached into my pocket. "I probably shouldn't have stolen this, then."

"What the hell is that?"

I opened my hand which held a jewel the size of a walnut.

"Is that a diamond?"

June 19, 1956: Yuma, Arizona

"Are you seeing this?" I asked.

**He's a monster**. Adam's voice answered inside my head.

"The ground just swallowed Beijing and everyone in it."

**A sociopath with a Talent. Thank God it didn't happen before the Great War.**

"Can you imagine this guy running around the states? If the Japanese had him during the war, there wouldn't be a United States anymore."

"Very true," he said as he walked down the stairs. "I'm going to grab some groceries."

I waved in his direction as he took the keys for the Bel Air from the keyring holder.

"You know they're calling it a Bend, now," I said.

"It's a stupid name but I bet it sticks."

"I kind of like it," I said. "B.E.N.T."

"Of course you do. I hate it, so obviously you're going to like it."

I laughed. "Will you bring back some RC?"

"Sure thing."

I was waiting for a guy who could sell the huge diamond for me, or I would have gone with him. How I wished I had gone with him. I wouldn't see my brother for two years after that day.

## November 14, 1958: Prescott, Arizona

There was a small overlook where I watched the movement around the warehouse. My connection said it was a black site for the CIA which meant there would be serious defenses around the place. The Central Intelligence Agency hadn't really become a large organization until the asteroid fell. It grew exponentially over the following years.

Two years and close to a million dollars went into the search for Adam. The last of my funds from selling the diamond was spent, but this one was a good lead. They were rumored to be holding him in this warehouse. More accurately, in the compound below it. Between the lead itself and the blueprints for the underground complex, I was dead broke. But Adam was there. I could feel it. I could feel him.

I slid back down from the overlook and opened the trunk of the Bel Air.

"Sorry about all this, Doc." I patted the restrained man's shoulder. "Y'all got my brother in there and I'm going to need your face."

My features melted and took on the likeness of the man in the trunk. His eyes widened in alarm.

"If he's unhurt, I won't hurt anyone when this goes down."

I took his security badge and shut the trunk. Then I got into the driver's seat of the Plymouth he had been driving and drove right in the front gate like Doctor Phillip Frye did every other day. No one suspected a thing. I was able to walk right into what they claimed was the most secure facility in the country.

In the fifth sub-basement, I found Adam. He was rail thin and there were scars on the side of his head where they had cut him open.

"I kn..new you'd find me," he stuttered. "I s…see y..you've got your… talent under control."

"Yep." I embraced my brother. "What have they done to you? Never mind. You can tell me later. Let's get you out of here."

We made it back up to the warehouse level before they realized I wasn't taking him for another "experiment" as the doctor had done many times. The bullets began to fly. I shielded Adam with my body which I had hardened so it could block the incoming fire.

We were at the door when it opened, and a young agent opened fire from there. I was behind Adam and couldn't shield him in time. As bullets rocked him, Adam stumbled. The agent screamed and grabbed his head.

I caught Adam and held him in my arms as the light drained from his eyes.

**I'm sorry** were the last words I heard in my mind as bullets hit me from almost everywhere.

"What happened after is not important," I said.

Bets was looking at me in horror. "They had cut into his head to study his Bend?"

"They cut into his head to remove it. His Bend was nearly gone but he still said that in my mind. Why would he be sorry? I didn't get him out. It wasn't his fault. I didn't want to kill anyone, so I tried to sneak out. I should have just killed them all. I ended up killing them all anyway."

"That's not what the history books say."

"Yeah, they labeled me as a terrorist. They've been trying to find me ever since."

"When I was done, I found forty-six other people in that base with scars that had been lobotomized. They find telepaths and they cut it out of their brains along with whatever it takes with it. How Adam had anything left at all I'll never understand."

"I never believed…"

"Now you've seen. You need to get the hell out of the city. If they find you, it's all over. Kelen can get you clear of this place." I looked at Kelen. "Give her the escape package we set up for Belize. I can spare a couple of them anyway."

"The whole package?"

"Minus your cut," I said. "I don't expect you to work for free. Give her the package and make sure she never comes back."

"Honey, you have a generous heart. You don't even know her."

"I know what they'll do to her, and that's enough."

I glanced at the telepath who just sat there in a daze as it really set in what kind of foe she faced. "You'll be safe there."

I turned away and walked out of the safe room in a red dress that clung to Sophia Ritten's body like a second layer of skin. I pulled a rolling suitcase with seven other outfits for the various identities I would be using over the next few weeks.

Stepping out of the hair salon, I smiled as a cab swung to the curb. When you wear a body like Sophia's it drew attention.

"Airport, sugah," I said in a southern accent.

"Yes, Ma'am."

# Chapter 5

I left the airport in New York and easily caught a cab. Sophia hadn't let me down. It's so much easier to get help when you're beautiful. But you're also noticed by everyone. It's hard to do covert shit when you look like a movie star.

Fortunately, that is exactly what I was after. I needed Sophia to get seen.

"Addams Grand please," I said in her southern accent.

The swarthy driver nodded and merged into traffic like he was a NASCAR driver.

We stopped in front of an old Hotel that had been quite elegant in its day. It still had that old charm but some of the neighboring areas had lost ground to the urban sprawl. There was more of the worst side of the BENT around this part of the city. Deformities abound in parts of the city. Back before the asteroid changed everything, there was a series of comic books about a vigilante who dressed as a bat and fought crime in a fictional city called Gotham. This part of New York reminded me of the comic. It was dark and dangerous. But there was no batman policing the night.

I tipped the cabbie and walked into the Grand pulling the suitcase. I made sure that Sophia Ritten was seen checking into room 721. When the doors were locked, I stripped off the dress and the tiny undergarments. Didn't need to shift into Seamus with that get-up on.

"Shame," I said looking into the mirror. "You're a lot prettier than he is."

Concentrating, my features moved around, and I watched the reflection begin to take shape. "Fuckin leprechaun," I said with a chuckle.

Kelen was full of shit, but he was probably the best friend I had in this world. And he did some spectacular work. All seven of the IDs he'd created for me went so deep, they would pass any government background check. There was not a computer in the world Kelen couldn't manipulate. If it was on the net, he could go there. If it was in a building with electricity, he could travel there. Even the "secure" buildings with internal servers still took electricity to run. They couldn't keep him out if he wanted in.

When I met him, he was a street kid, and his Bend hadn't manifested. The kid was smart and one of the best pickpockets I'd ever seen. I stopped some thugs from beating on him and he showed me around Chicago. I sent him to a private school and on to college where he discovered his talent.

He never forgot about what I did for him, and he was the one person I could trust with everything. He had put together quite a few escape packages for me over the years where I would go into hiding if it got too hot for me.

So far, I hadn't needed one for myself. I gave the one to Bets because I couldn't stand to see what they would do to her. She was still young enough to have that naivety that I didn't want to see destroyed.

I'd given another to Jasper. He was the guy who took me under his wing after the thing in Arizona. He taught me about the game and kept me out of the trouble my rage would have had me in. He was now working on his second century and living on an island in the Caribbean.

I shook my head and pulled the clothes from the suitcase. After donning the clothes, I took a small camera from the case. It had a three-foot lead with the lens on the end. I slipped it just under the edge of the door and panned it from right to left. There was a couple about to enter their room, but the hall was empty as soon as they stepped in.

Pitching the camera to the side of the door, I stood and exited. Stopping in the hall I leaned against the wall until one of the hotel staff passed. Having been seen I could go on and leave. I needed my story to check out when they looked into it. The Kazaskis wouldn't just take the word of a stranger. I made sure I was seen in the lobby and on the street in front by several folks.

Walking down the street, I shook my head. There were a lot of BENT in this part of the city. Most were on the lower end of the power spectrum. Some received a genuine talent and others were just BENT. Lillana, the bartender would be on the lower spectrum, but her Bend was fairly harmless. Many were deformed in ways that would make a person, well… shake their head.

There was a man with four tentacles where each arm should have been. The tentacles were of varying length from about four feet long to a little under two feet. At least they were long enough to still be useful. He was holding a bag with what looked like a bottle of bourbon in one of the tentacles.

Further along, a woman slithered along the sidewalk. Her lower half was a serpent.

These were the ones that stood out the most, but I would get glimpses of red eyes or odd shades of skin in the people moving along the streets. Society still considered us as sub-human in most cases.

Then there were the Talents. I wouldn't be seeing them down here in the streets. They would be in the much nicer side of the city. People like Solomon Gold. He was literally gold-plated. His dandruff was worth money. There were a few like him that were just rich because of their Bend.

Then there were the heroes like Deborah Diamond. With super strength and impenetrable skin, she fought crime in a skimpy outfit like in the old comics. There weren't as many of the "heroes" around once the city demanded that they pay for the damage they caused. Hero insurance was costly, and it took a lot of money to live that life.

More and more, the smaller cities were following the example set by New York. They'd regret it in the future was my opinion because a world with the ability to have superheroes also has supervillains. They don't give one shit about the damage done. The heroes were the one thing keeping the villains from running rampant. I figured we'd see a lot more problems over the next few years.

I spotted the place I was looking for called "The No Holes Barred" and shook my head again. This whore house that was supposed to *just* be a strip club was definitely not a venerable establishment like the one Kelen ran some years ago. The sign was in a livid neon red with a neon pole dancer.

I chuckled as I stepped inside. "Bet he'd have a few words to say about it."

According to the information packet he'd given me before I left, the Kazaskis owned this and several more across the city.

I stopped just inside and let my eyes roam the inside of the club. The dancer on the center stage caught my attention. She reminded me of Evangeline. Where Evangeline's had been the purest white, *her* wings were ebony colored and reflected the light with their glossy sheen. Her skin was close to the same shade, and she had tattoos across her body in a scarlet red. Long red hair flowed around her as she danced. I was duly impressed.

Her Bend would be considered a talent if she were modeling for the wealthy. Here, she was the draw that filled the club every night. Perhaps I was judging the place too harshly. Kelen would have killed to have her as his main attraction.

"Wonder what she's doing here, then," I muttered.

I understood a little better when she finished her act to the cheers of the crowd. Two men I had assumed were bouncers stepped on the stage and she folded her wings in, tucking in at her sides. She proceeded them into the back and one of the others cleaned up the money scattered across the stage.

"Bet she doesn't see any of that," I said under my breath.

The guys I thought were there to protect her looked more like they were her guards. The Kazaskis had more to answer for than Gwen Krimoni, the girl I was looking for. I hated slavery more than anything and human trafficking was all about slavery.

The winged dancer was BENT, and people didn't seem to care what happened to the BENT. They cheered and threw money on the stage.

I sighed and turned away. "One thing at a time," I said softly.

Several drinks later, I was talking to the bartender as another dancer took to the stage. She was beautiful and a great dancer, but she was nowhere near the same league as her predecessor. But she was fully human and left the stage with the money she had earned and no guards to keep her in line.

"Man, you wouldn't believe the chick I saw at the Grand…"

# Chapter 6

They came for me three days later. Or rather, they came for Sophia. In those three days, she had been out of the hotel a few times shopping for clothes and eating at relatively decent restaurants. She kept to herself and left the impression of sadness behind.

She had no family left and no one else in her life, now. Her background was impeccable and Kelen had called as soon as the first search had gone through. She was the perfect victim. No one would miss her.

There were three of them who grabbed me in the night, and I smelled the sweet smell of chloroform. A normal would be out for hours but I could drink that crap if I wanted. I feigned unconsciousness as they stood around the bed.

"Damn, this one's hot as hell." I felt hands where they shouldn't be, and it took a lot of patience not to cut off parts of the three men.

They removed the night clothes I was wearing, and I thought they were going to go further but the apparent leader stopped the other two. "Time enough for that when we get back to Halleck's."

"Probably right," the one who'd commented first said, giving my ass a squeeze. "Oh, what I'm going to do to you."

*Oh, what I'm going to do to you,* I thought.

They put a hood over my head and dumped me in a laundry cart, naked. Laundry was stripped from the bed and my Sophia clothes were thrown into the cart on top of me. The suitcase was next and the bed linens last to cover me up.

I thought about killing them, but I would have to interrogate them for the location of their base of operations. I assumed they would probably just take me there as a captive. Plenty of time for killing once we got there. I hate slavery. Did I already say that?

"The boss might want to keep this one for the club. She's got the whole package."

"He'll let us play some first," another voice said.

I gritted my teeth as they pushed the cart out the door. Sometimes restraint is the hardest thing in my line of business. I would almost rather do the whole interrogation thing. I was fairly certain I was going to kill some people very soon.

"Speaking of that," the leader said. "Boss said I could have Twilight for the weekend after bringing him the lead on this."

"No shit?" the first voice I had heard asked.

"The freak?" came from the third. He was the guy who had commented on the things he would do to me.

"Freak or not, she's mine for the weekend."

"You can have her," he said. "I got nothin' for any of those freaks except my boot."

"Better not let Halleck hear that."

"He's one of the freaks," the guy said.

"Like to see you try to put the boot to him," Leader laughed. "He'd tear you in half."

"This place was a lot better before that freak got mixed up with it."

"I'm not gonna argue that," Leader said. "But we do get to sample most of the goods before they go on to wherever he sees fit to use them."

It was a relief when they wheeled the cart into a box truck and shut the door. Every one of these guys deserved what was coming. I was worried about Halleck, though. If he was a Talent, it might be a problem.

The ride wasn't as long as I expected. I really thought they would be based further out but I wasn't complaining. The sooner we got there, the sooner I could end this charade.

The cart was wheeled out of the truck and across concrete floors. I could hear and feel the roughness under the wheels.

They dumped me out of the laundry cart abruptly and one of them grabbed me around the waist to throw me onto a table. "She's heavy."

"I've been waiting for this part," Freak hater said and rubbed up against me.

My hands melted through the ties that had been around them and I pulled the hood from my head.

"Oh, I've been waiting for this part too, sugah," I said in Sophia's southern drawl.

The hater took a step back with a scowl. It turned to a look of terror as I turned to face him with glowing red eyes and a wide smile of needle-sharp teeth.

"Is this the reception all the girls get, or is this the *special* treatment?"

"What the hell are you?" Leader asked. I recognized the voice coming from the tall muscular bald man.

"Don't you think I'm pretty?" I asked and protruded a twelve-inch tongue.

Hater scrambled for a gun he'd left on a table beside him when he removed his belt to take a turn on Sophia. For some reason, he didn't seem to want to continue.

"Oh, don't do that, sugah," I said as I jumped forward and wrapped my arms around him.

I threw him aside and picked up the pistol. With a few deft moves, I popped the magazine out and stripped the gun, letting it fall to the floor.

The Leader had his pistol out and fired a single shot into my chest which passed through my malleable body without harm.

I raised my hands and blades grew from the tips of my fingers. "Playing rough." I shrugged. "That's okay too."

Neither of the two had time to do much more than yelp as my blades sliced through them. I looked at number three who was frozen with a look of pure terror on his face.

"That just leaves little old you to answer my questions." I was next to him in an instant with a bladed finger sliding down his cheek.

"Wh…what do you want to kn…now?"

A second blade touched skin. "Everything. Tell me everything and I may let you live."

Annoyed with Lloyd

# Chapter 7

It hurt my heart to leave the bastard alive after all the women he had abused along with his cohorts. Apparently, it was a regular thing for them. At least he wouldn't be doing that anymore. Not after certain parts were removed and cauterized. I said I would let him live, not that it would be a happy existence. He deserved worse but I needed to get the girls out of the warehouse before Halleck returned.

He was indeed a Talent. Super strength and impenetrable scales that covered his body made him someone it would be difficult to handle. I was almost certain I'd seen someone like him fighting with one of the Talents years ago. They destroyed a lot of property. If it was the same guy, I didn't want to have anything to do with him.

The hall I was in led into the warehouse proper where all the girls were kept. The large warehouse had lines of rooms along the outside walls. At least they weren't cages.

"What are you doin' out here? You should be in your room." A tall red-haired man said as he saw me.

He hadn't seen the blood on the front of the shirt I had stolen from Baldy. It was long enough to be a dress on Sophia.

I ran straight toward him, and the blades flashed. I was pulling no punches. These men were making slaves of women and I was going to end it. I found seven men inside the warehouse guarding the prisoners and dispatched the last of them just in time for Halleck to arrive.

He was close to seven feet tall and silvery scales covered his arms and face. Presumably, they covered his entire body.

"That's about enough of that, Lassie," he said with a Scottish accent.

"I'm just getting' started, sugah."

I slashed at him, and sparks flew as the blades scraped across his chest, shredding the shirt. He caught my right arm and yanked me back to face him instead of sweeping by as I had planned.

"Shit."

"What did ye expect? I cannae be harmed by those shiny toys. I'm a Talent."

My hand slipped from his grasp as I concentrated a moment and let it melt.

"What the Hell?"

"Not your regular prey this time," I said in a deeper voice without the accent.

He swung a punch at me that sank almost all the way through my chest. I kept my body malleable, so he was punching into a sponge. It still hurt but there was no serious damage.

Stepping back from him I continued, "If you let 'em go, I'll let you live."

I already knew the answer to that. I just needed a little time to do the shifts necessary for what I would have to do. This guy was a Talent. There was no way he thought for an instant I could hurt him. Arrogance was their stock in trade.

As he laughed at my statement, I leapt forward. He caught me by the neck, just like he expected. What he didn't expect was the lower half of my body wrapping around his head. Both legs and arms encircled his head and pulled my body tightly to his face.

He pulled at my neck, but it just stretched. Dropping that grip he clawed at his face as his airways filled. My body stretched as he pulled, and it took all of my concentration to hold to the form

I had settled into. I stretched like taffy when he grasped parts and pulled.

Keeping my concentration was grueling. It didn't work as easily as it used to, and this guy was strong as hell. Every time he pulled it hurt but I couldn't do anything about it. Five full minutes he struggled before it was over. I had lost concentration a few times and bones had snapped. It was a massive relief, and I was dizzy when I released my grip from around his head.

"I'm a Talent, too, you prick."

Dragging myself away from the dead Talent, I eased my back against the wall of one of the rooms and tried to focus on the leg bone that had been broken. Then the left arm. They fused back together slowly.

A decade ago, I never would have lost the concentration needed to keep it from happening. Now I leaned against a wall in an old man's body trying to keep my eyes open long enough to heal a few bones.

A shadow moved from the darkness at the other end of the room, and I saw an angel.

"Beautiful…" I muttered just before I passed out.

I awoke in a bed with what felt like every muscle and joint hurting. It took a lot to handle the stress of having your body stretched by someone with super strength. Everything hurt afterward. I concentrated and began shifting, repairing my body.

As the pain eased, I could take a moment to look around. It looked like the room I had been in at the Addams Grand.

"I found your key in the stuff they had at the loading dock."

My head snapped to the left where the woman I assumed was called Twilight sat perched on the front of the chair. Her glossy black wings were spread wide.

"I haven't been able to spread my wings in over a year," she said. Her voice was deeper than I had expected but it was also velvety soft.

"They had you that long?" I asked with a raspy voice. An old man's voice.

I started shifting, my body filling out with a younger man's physique.

"You're him, aren't you? I thought you were just a myth. The one they still talk about nearly a century later."

"Not sure who you're talking about," I said.

"One side claims a terrorist and a murderer. The other, a hero and savior."

I grunted as my face shifted into the third of my identities, Jerome Falcone. He was a notorious gambler… according to his background.

"You are the one named Alexander Lloyd."

"Maybe a little of both those things, and a lot of neither."

"I think more of the savior and less of the murderer," she said. "You saved thirty-six women yesterday."

"One of them wouldn't be named Gwen Krimoni, would it?"

"Not at the warehouse." Her wings flexed and pulled in behind her back, the tops curving two feet above her shoulders. "She is currently being held at the club. More accurately, in the penthouse above the club. Patrick Kazaski has shown a liking for her, and his father gave Gwen to him."

"Looks like it's time to burn it down after all."

She stood and her wings spread again. "Is there anything I can do to help?"

"Yeah, I think there is. And you're gonna love it."

# Chapter 8

I had a hard time keeping my eyes on the target instead of Twilight. She wore a tank top cut extra low in the back to go under her wings. With that much cut out of it, the shirt hung loosely.

"Dirty old man," I muttered.

"You've seen everything already," she said with a grin. "You said you were in the club when I danced."

"I was distracted then, too." I pointed from the ledge of the building we were standing atop. "When you want to hurt someone like the Kazaskis you have to know what they do. They specialize in drugs and gambling. My friend tells me they have a ton of money in banks all over the world. He's going to take care of that. That building across the way has the bulk of their physical cash reserves in a vault on the top floor."

"I like where this is going."

"Yep, we're going to take it. I'd like for you to meet me on the roof of that building when you see my signal."

"And what will your signal be?"

I showed her what I had in the bag sitting beside me. "Oh, you'll know the signal."

"That looks like C4."

"You've seen it before?"

"I have. Seems like a lifetime ago, though."

"Curiouser and curiouser," I said.

"I have only been their captive for a little over a year."

"How did they keep you from escaping?"

"Halleck pinned my wings where I could not extend them. The most movement I have had for them has been while I dance. They were pinned immediately after my act." She bent her wings in where I could see the spot where the clamps had been kept on the ridges of both wings.

"Fuckin' assholes."

"Yes."

"How much weight can you carry while flying?"

"I can carry a person if it isn't far. Perhaps two hundred for short distances."

"Damn," I said and pulled the shirt off I wore.

Closing my eyes, I envisioned the shift, and black wings sprouted from my back. My skin turned black, and I lost a foot in height.

"Dumnezeu!"

I opened my eyes and looked at her.

"God," she said. "I am Romanian. Sometimes it comes out and *this* I did not expect."

"I can fly like this but can't carry much. To keep my size and add these the mass comes from somewhere. I can't change that."

"I will carry whatever you need," she said.

"Remember, wait 'til the signal before flying over."

"I will wait."

I kept the shirt in my hand and the small bag in the other as I leapt over the edge and flapped the wings to keep me aloft. I landed on the roof of Kazaski's headquarters and concentrated again, shifting back into the form I had used on the other building. Putting the shirt back on, I examined the roof.

"Bingo," I said as I spied the machinery shed for the elevator.

I flattened my hand and slid it under the door. Then I pushed more under to turn up and unlock the door. I took the small bag and stepped inside, shutting and locking the door behind me. I thought I would have to cut my way into the elevator shaft, but the maintenance door was unlocked. It made climbing into the shaft a lot simpler.

Climbing down the maintenance ladder kept me in a groove that the elevator wouldn't reach if someone inside used it. I spent almost a whole hour setting the small C4 charges throughout the building with detonators. They would make a lot of noise which was the idea. I wasn't interested in killing them.

I climbed back up the shaft and waited for the elevator to pass me as it climbed.

"Time to rock and roll." I pulled the tiny transmitter and pushed the button.

There were twelve small bombs timed to go off in a sequence that would keep everyone busy. There was a rumble as the first one went off down in the elevator shaft. I didn't want them using it. Alarms were going off in the main areas of the building and People would be evacuating pretty soon. Especially after number two went off a few moments later. I gave them a few minutes and dropped into the elevator from the emergency hatch.

The open door button worked and I peeked out of the elevator. No one was in sight, so I strolled down the hall to the room with the vault.

Placing a bud in my ear and tapping the button I said, "Cameras, Kel."

"They're out. You're not workin' with amateurs, here."

"Heh."

There was another thump as the third of my surprises detonated.

The vault was unguarded, and I leaned on the wall. "Anytime."

"You do realize I'm three thousand miles away, right?"

"Excuses, excuses."

The electric locks triggered. "Kiss my ass."

I chuckled and pulled the door open. "Damn. That's a lot of cash."

I pulled the last items from my small bag and dropped the bag onto the floor. Two of them were medium-sized gym bags and the third was a road flare. After filling the first bag, I saw the stack of Swiss bearer bonds on the shelf. They went into the other bag, and I filled it the rest of the way with stacks of bills.

Setting them to the side, I pulled the rest of the cash off of the shelves and threw in a few of the bonds close to the edge. Striking the flare, I threw it onto the pile of money and picked up the duffels. They were about seventy-five pounds each. Probably about six or seven million. The bonds, on the other hand, were a hundred thousand apiece. There was a stack of them. Another fifteen million I would guess.

As the next two packages detonated, I walked out onto the roof from the stairs. Twilight crouched near the maintenance shed and smiled as I set the two duffels down in front of her.

"I almost expected you to take the building down," she said as she lifted the bags.

"If I killed them, they wouldn't learn anything."

Removing my shirt, my wings sprouted again, and I dropped in height.

We both leapt upward and with strong beats of our wings, rose into the night.

"Now I go after Gwen," I said. "They'll be distracted for a while."

"We."

"I figured you'd want to haul ass with the money. That's why I took it. They owe you for what you went through."

"I'll still take their money," she said. "But we will free your girlfriend, first."

"She's not my girlfriend, she's my client's daughter."

"Ah, I see. You are a mercenary?"

"Not really, I like to hurt bad people, and sometimes I can help someone in the process."

"Then let's help someone and afterwards, we will celebrate."

"Sounds like a plan to me."

Surprisingly enough, finding and removing Gwen from the club was simple as walking in and walking out. Several hours after we left the almost empty club, Gwen was on a plane to LA where her father lived.

The celebrating... well, that took much longer. Several weeks, in fact.

Annoyed with Lloyd

# Chapter 9

I stepped in the door with a duffel bag.

"I'll be right with you, sweetie… oh, it's you." Kelen frowned.

"Don't be so enthusiastic about it," I said.

"You don't come through this often unless there's a problem."

"Or if I have a present for you."

"Are we about to be in a gunfight?"

"Not that kind of present," I replied. I handed Kelen the duffel. "Good presents."

He laid it on a counter and opened the bag. "Hmm."

"Figured you might do something about those."

"Someone would have to go to Switzerland unless you want them fenced."

"Either is good."

"Here, we'll get maybe fifty cents on the dollar."

"It's up to you."

"For an extra eight million dollars, I'll go to Switzerland."

"Great."

He lowered the bag to the floor behind the counter. "They're saying America's most wanted terrorist was sighted in New York. You're usually a little more careful than this."

"Ran into a Talent. The guy was a handful and I'm not as spry as I used to be."

"Word is that he was seen in his natural form. You never lose that much control, even asleep."

"I told you, he was a handful. It took everything I had. I hate dealing with Talents."

"You should have run," he said.

"Couldn't leave those girls trapped there. It was shit timing. If he'd been ten minutes later, we'd have been gone."

"I looked him up. He went toe to toe with the Paladin in 2012."

"Yep."

"You aren't supposed to be fighting Talents like that, sweetie." He stared at me for a full minute. "You should retire. Go live on an island like your friend, Jasper."

"I'd be bored to death," I said with a shrug. "I spent the last three weeks with a Romanian angel. How could an island retirement compare to that?"

"Where's your dark angel, now?"

I sighed. "She went back home with a duffel bag full of cash. She'll probably buy a castle."

"And of course, she didn't ask you to go."

I shrugged.

"Figures."

She did ask me to go but that fight with Halleck had opened my eyes. When I'd come to and saw what my body really was underneath the Talent, I realized I was still on a timer and that it was probably getting pretty close to running out. Sure, I was probably the healthiest ninety-three-year-old man in the world, but I was still an old man. I might have twenty years left or I might have two.

"You got a guard for a trip to Switzerland? I know a guy that creates shields. He could escort."

"I might just take you up on that."

I picked up a pen and wrote a number on a post-it. "He's one of the good ones."

"Since you won't retire," he said with a shake of his head. "There's a job one of my sources gave to me. They asked for you, personally. Some sort of private club in Portland. Talents."

"I don't know. I don't like Talents."

He raised one eyebrow.

"Most Talents."

"Honey, I hate the bastards, but you *did* just give away an estate in Belize. You might want to consider it."

I pointed at the bag behind the counter.

"That's already spent," he said.

"What?"

"You're the proud owner of a new jet. Now you won't be flying coach anymore, and more importantly, *I* won't be flying coach anymore."

"I see how it is. A minute ago, you wanted me to retire." I chuckled.

"I already knew you wouldn't."

"Give me what you have on 'em before you leave."

"They have surprisingly little in the ether about them and a very good computer guy. I wouldn't be surprised if they had a Talent like yours truly working for them."

"I didn't know there were any Talents like you, Kel."

"There are several of us swimming around and we stay out of each other's ponds. I may not be able to help on this one, my friend."

"That's fine. Go get the money to pay for the damn jet. I think I'll drive up to Portland. I haven't driven anywhere in a while."

"Weren't you just all over New York State?"

I smiled. "We flew."

"You really liked this one, didn't you?"

"Maybe," I said and turned to leave. "Be careful. They may be watching for someone coming to cash those in."

"The Kazaskis? They're not watching a damn thing. After losing all that money, they had another run of bad luck. Seems they were laundering for some cartels."

"Cartels?"

"Seems they didn't like the Kazaskis after that. You know how the cartels are."

"I'm guessing the Kazaskis quietly disappeared?"

"Something like that."

"Hmmf."

"I don't sense any sympathy."

"When they started trafficking in young girls, I lost all sympathy."

"Me too."

I stepped out the door and turned left toward the warehouse district. I needed a car.

# Chapter 10

"He's in Vegas," one of the passengers on the bus said.

I glanced over. She was a twenty-something, bouncy brunette sitting with a male version of the same person.

"I wish we could have seen him while he was here," he replied.

I just shook my head and tuned them out. The Japanese Emperor was the last person I was interested in meeting.

The bus would run close to the warehouses, and I would walk the rest of the way. A woman in her forties sat across the aisle from me. She gasped as she watched her phone.

"Oh my god," she said and turned toward me. "Have you seen the latest in internet challenges?"

"I hate those things," I said shaking my head.

"You remember the guy in Frisco that was committing suicide last week?"

"I've been out of town for a month or so."

"He jumped from a building and wanted to stop it halfway down. There was a big thing about it on the news. It went nationwide."

"I was out of touch for a bit. Doesn't seem like a jumper would go nationwide."

"No, it sparked a Talent as he was falling, and he *flew!*"

"Ah, that would explain it."

"I wish it hadn't gone out to the whole world," she said. "Now they're doing this Blue-Tube challenge about it."

"Don't tell me kids are jumping off buildings."

"They're screaming 'Let's get BENT!' and trying to trigger a talent."

"Idiots." I grimaced. "At least it should be a short-lived challenge. It's a gruesome end if it doesn't work."

"Why would they do it? I just don't understand it."

"You'll never understand the next generation. I think it's in the rule book."

"You're probably right. My kids keep me baffled. At least they won't do anything like this. They already have talents. I guess they call themselves BENT. Thank God they were just small Bends."

"Some of them get lucky that way."

"My daughter has a different pigmentation, multi-colored, like a rainbow. Her twin brother is in greyscale. They had to deal with a lot of crap in school, so I pulled them out and sent them to Valenwood."

"Ah, the school for the BENT. I've heard of it. I knew one of the teachers some time back." I stood up. "This is my stop. You have a nice day ma'am. I'd stop looking at the news. It's always the worst in us that they try to put on display."

"You're right there. Thanks for the conversation. It's usually lacking on the bus line."

I smiled and made my way to the front. Stepping off the bus, I turned toward the west. My warehouse was down close to the docks. It wasn't a huge warehouse like many of them, but it was old. I'd bought it in the sixties. I walked for about a half hour before rounding a corner and stopping in my tracks.

There were cops everywhere and the doors to my building were open wide.

"Fuck."

I turned and stepped back around the corner. In the next two miles, I shifted three times and tossed my coat in a trash can. I bought a ball cap in the first store I came across and a pay-as-you-go cell phone. I dialed a number Kelen would be sure to answer.

"What happened?" was the answer.

"Warehouse is burnt," I said. "Crawling with cops. We need all ties to it cleaned up."

"I'll call you right back."

"Gotcha."

Normally he would have given me a ration of shit for keeping the stuff there, but he had been in a hurry. He gave me hell for keeping the Bel Air more than anything else.

It was a '55 and it belonged to my brother. It was the last thing I had that had been his and I couldn't bring myself to get rid of it. There were other cars in the warehouse but that one had a clear link to me. The others were registered to various identities I had used over the years. They would be cleaned by Kelen now that they were burned.

What could I say? I liked cars. Some of them, I liked well enough to keep.

Fifteen minutes passed before the phone rang.

"Yep."

"Sweetie. How many times did I tell you to get rid of the cars?"

"Too many."

"And *now* you see why."

"Yeah."

I could even see the disapproving look on his face that I knew was there.

"Bought you a car two blocks from where you're at. Use the Falcone ID." He was quiet for a moment. "I'm sorry about the Bel Air."

"It was bound to happen sooner or later."

"Still sucks."

"It'll be fun stealing it back."

"What?" I could hear his head bobbing through the phone. "Oh, you did *not* just say steal it back."

"Well, not *today*," I said. "But I'll steal it back."

"That car will be the most heavily guarded vehicle in the world."

"I know. Right?"

He sighed. "Just pick up the Cadillac from Wheelers and get the hell out of LA."

"Kicking me out, huh?"

"Absolutely. LA and New York are both too hot for you. Maybe Portland will be better."

"Better than what? Portland sucks."

"How would you know? It's been thirty years since you were there."

"It sucked then."

"Just go," he said. "And be careful. Keep your head down."

"Alright, I'll try."

"I guess that's as good as I can expect. I'm leaving for Switzerland tomorrow. If you need me, call this phone."

"Gotcha. I'll just plan for a leisurely trip up the coast. Might stop in Frisco on the way."

"Just be careful."

"You already said that."

"I really meant it."

# Chapter 11

San Francisco was a pretty good sized city and a large portion was still under construction. Re-construction, to be more accurate. Three years back a couple of Superman-level types went through the place and made one hell of a mess. I remembered reading comics about Superman for years before the asteroid hit and made it fact instead of fiction.

Only thing was, people aren't as noble as the guy in the comics. When the damage was done, both of the Talents were caught and tried in court. Both were found guilty of more counts of manslaughter than any other criminal previously captured.

You might wonder how they were captured. Frisco put a new task force together in 2017. They called themselves the SFPDTRF. Too much of the alphabet in an acronym, if you asked me. San Francisco Police Department Talent Reaction Force, or Reaction Force for short. It was the first of its kind and I expected the other cities to follow suit. New York was right on the verge of setting one up and Los Angeles was talking about it as well.

The one in Frisco had a group of Talents working for the city alongside a bunch of regular cops. They were the ones who stopped Killjoy and Belgrave when they were on their tear. One of the TRF was a Talent they called White Noise. He could project this haze of noise and light that would put someone out in a few minutes.

I was always careful to keep my head down in Frisco and most of the Talents were civil when they were in town. The TRF wouldn't come for you if you stayed out of trouble. They'd probably make an exception for the guy on the top ten boards in every agency.

Why was I going there? It was where Donny was living in the retirement home. Donny was a guy I met probably fifty years back when I stole his car. Thing is, Donny is a Talent. He made quite a living as a guy everyone called the Finder. He could find anything if he wanted to find it. He found me in less than an hour after I took his Dodge Charger. Instead of turning me in, he hired me to work for him. I spent a little over ten years working as twelve different assistants. Each would stay for a year or so and be replaced with another. It may have been the steadiest time of my life.

Donny was in bad shape and every time I came by, I thought it might be the last. Donny LeBraun was ninety-eight years old, and he hadn't lived the easiest life. He always treated me like his kid even if I was only a few years younger than he was. I don't remember if I ever even told him that. I was content being his "kid" after he retired. I kept an eye on the payments and took over when his bank ran dry. He didn't even know about that. I shifted before I turned into the lot for Green Valley Retirement Home. I had been playing Donny's son for more than a few years and came to see him every six months or so. On each visit I aged just a little so they wouldn't get suspicious.

I didn't need to swap clothes because Falcone was the same size or fairly close to Jimmy LeBraun. The suit fit just fine. Parking the Escalade, I made my way to the entry and stopped at the desk.

"LeBraun," I said.

"Oh dear," the pretty brunette behind the desk replied.

I could already figure out what she was about to say.

"I'm so sorry, Mister LeBraun. He passed two days ago. I think they've been trying to contact you."

"I've been out of touch for a bit." My disappointment was quite obvious. "You said a couple days?"

"Yes, sir. I am truly sorry for your loss. Let me go get Mister Holiday. He's the head of staff during the week."

I nodded and sat down in one of the comfortable chairs against the wall. I guess I was right the last time. I looked around and thought about what it would be like to settle down in a place like this. Just rest. Unfortunately, I couldn't retire like any regular person. I was always hunted. If I stayed in one place too long, I would make a mistake, and someone would be looking to get rich quick.

I would have to use one of the escape packages Kelen had built for me and stay the hell away from people when I decided to retire. I mean, they're really nice places so I won't be uncomfortable, but I would miss life. Like sleeping with a bearded lady or carousing the state of New York with my Twilight Angel. I really enjoyed spending time with her, even with her knowing who I was. She just enjoyed being free again and wasn't after anything from me except my company.

We had spent three days in bed at Niagara Falls just ordering room service and enjoying each other. But there was always that memory of me when I woke up as a heavy set ninety-three-year-old man. How could I justify doing that to her? I could be gone any time.

The depression I felt could be from things like this where I watch people I knew dying of old age. How long could I really get by with the shapeshifting keeping me young? I assumed that if I did what I did to Halleck after a little more time there wouldn't be anything left but a dried-out husk.

Best to avoid Talents. Yet here I was on my way to Portland to meet a group of them for a job.

A short, balding man in an expensive suit entered the lobby and extended his hand toward me. "My condolences, Mister LeBraun. I know this has just been laid in your lap but there is some final paperwork for you to fill out if you can. I will most certainly understand if you need a few days."

"It's okay," I said. "I've been expecting something like this for years. We can get everything straight today."

"Please follow me, then."

Entering the old storage facility, I had to wonder what Donny had kept squirreled away. He'd left a will that gave everything to me including a key to a storage unit. It wasn't far from the spot where White Noise had taken down the two Talents. It was a stroke of luck it hadn't been demolished. The place was climate controlled, and his unit was all the way on the top floor.

"What did you keep in storage, old friend?"

The key fit a regular lock that actually looked out of place in the line of round locks designed not to be cut by bolt cutters.

"If you use elaborate locks people assume you have expensive shit." I chuckled remembering him saying that to me what seemed like a thousand years ago.

I slid the door up and turned on the light. I immediately closed the door behind me as I looked at the far wall, laughing.

"You old bastard," I muttered as I recognized a Van Gogh that had been missing for a long time.

The picture was of some yellow and red flowers. Beside it was a Raphael painting I remembered from a list of lost art. If I remembered correctly, all of these paintings hanging on the back wall were on that list and there were several stacked against the wall.

That wasn't all but they were the first things that caught my eye. Lost art, jewels, and a lot of unique items in a storage unit behind a ten-dollar lock. Apparently, Donny was right. You put a cheap lock on it, they didn't think anything worth a damn would be inside.

I figured he had just went looking for all the lost items that crossed his mind and thrown them in the unit. He would have found any of them for his regular fee, so I figured no one contracted for them. Donny, the guy I had been paying bills for over the last ten years might be one of the richest men in America.

I understood his message a little better now that I had seen the unit. The short note said, "Do with it what you please, kid, it might be one hell of a show."

I lost count of all that I found in the unit, but I stopped when I opened a small box with a note.

*I guess, if you're reading this, I'm gone, kid. Some of the best days of my life were spent working with you. Just for a lark, I went to find the first thing you ever stole. You started big, kid. See you on the other side!*

The item in the box was a diamond the size of a walnut and it was the only thing I took from the storage unit. I locked it back, shaking my head. The cops in Frisco were going to be making one hell of a find when I called it in from the Escalade. I could hear old Donny laughing like a madman inside my head. After the call, I destroyed the phone and threw it into the bay. Then I drove to a hotel just across the way and got a room facing the storage building.

No way was I missing the show. I sat out on the balcony and watched the first patrol car as it pulled in and a pair of deputies entered the facility. Pouring a glass of rum over some ice, I watched as more patrol cars arrived. In less than an hour, at least three flying Talents landed on the roof. I finished my rum and went inside for the bourbon, which was Donny's favorite.

Back outside on the balcony, I watched more cars and trucks arrive, then the black SUVs showed up.

"Feebs are here, Donny. Wish you could see the show." I raised my glass to the sky and took a long drink. It burned all the way down. "Gonna miss you down here brother. I'll see you soon enough."

The show lasted four days as people came from everywhere. It made National News with the price estimated in the billions. I could have kept it, but I think he knew what I'd do with it. I think he wanted it like this. He left one hell of a legacy behind. He was the Finder and he found anything he looked for. But the downside was if he thought about doing it, he would have to do it. That's how he had a storage unit with billions of dollars in lost treasures.

Annoyed with Lloyd

# Chapter 12

The drive up the coast was slow as I thought of my friend. Just one more that was gone. I didn't really have a lot of those who actually knew me left. There were people I had dealt with all over the country, but most had no idea I was *that* guy. The one with a ten-million-dollar bounty. They just knew one of my alter egos.

I could count the ones who knew who I was on the fingers of one hand until the last few months. Two more added, a telepath who should be in Belize by now and Twilight. There was one less now that Donny was gone.

My next stop was out in the middle of nowhere. It was in the Sequoya National Park. I rented a cabin for a couple of days with Grant Grove and hiked into the woods. The last time I was here was in 1956. Adam and I had come to see the giant redwoods shortly before he disappeared.

I trekked two hours into the forest before reaching the waterfall where I retraced the steps we had taken. I squatted looking at a redwood that towered above me.

"Damn you're old," I muttered to myself. "That was a sapling we placed in that spot. If you ever want to feel old, this is how you do it. Dumbass. Next thing you know you'll be drunk and crying."

I was right about the drunk part. I was drinking at a bar in one of the few lodges. The woman who ran the place had orange-tinted skin and flowers grew in her hair. She smelled of lavender and honey. She offered to drop me off at the cabin, but she ended up staying until morning. How could I retire to an island and miss days like this?

Portland had more BENT living in it than most cities. There was a reason I hadn't been back in thirty years. It was rife with crime. Funny as it sounds, with me on the most wanted list, I prefer places without riots and all the other stuff that came with the activists that clustered in Portland. It was unpleasant, at best.

In the last few years, the rampant destruction had lessened, whether it was due to the political climate or the fact that the group of Talents that wished to employ me had set up shop there I had no idea. I still hated to leave my car parked on the street and I was quite happy to see a valet service in front of the Elemental Club, where I was to meet with them.

Kelen had sent the Falcone identity to them as my contact.

"Jerome Falcone," I said to the valet as I handed him my keys.

He nodded. "They've been expecting you, sir."

"I didn't really specify when I was going to be here."

"It's been a standing order for close to a month, sir. It's good to see you here. They will be quite happy."

"Always better when the bosses are happy."

"Absolutely."

I chuckled and left the valet as he got into the seat I had vacated. The front of the place was elaborate with columns and stone stairs.

I sighed and went inside.

"Jerome Falcone," I said to the tuxedo-wearing man inside the entrance. "I think they're expecting me."

"Right you are, sir. If you will follow me, I will take you to the library. Master Khan will be there shortly."

"Alright."

I followed the grey-haired fellow down the hall to the right and into a large library with some pretty elaborate shelving. I'd seen a few places like this where the wealthy gathered, and robbed a few of them too. Many of the places like this screamed "old" money but were also "illegal" money and that was my target of choice under most circumstances.

I sat down in a comfortable seat that faced the door and still left a good view of the shelves that held leather-bound tomes. Some of them looked quite old, probably worth a great deal of money.

It wasn't long before a dark-haired man in an Armani suit walked into the library.

"Hello, Mister Falcone," he said with a greasy smile. That was the impression I got from him. Greasy, or something like that. "Or can we drop the pretense and say, Mister Lloyd?"

"We may both know it's a pretense, but it's for a reason. I'll stick with Falcone if you don't mind."

"That's just fine," he said. "As you say, it's there for a reason. Ten million reasons, you might say.

My name is Milo Khan, chairman of the Elemental Council. We would like to hire you, Mister… Falcone."

"That's what I've heard." I shrugged. "I'm here so it's safe to assume I'm interested."

"Then, by all means, join me. I'll introduce you to the council… Half of them, anyway. If we were aware, you would be here today all of us would have been sure to be present. Poor Virginia has been looking forward to meeting you."

"I try not to announce ahead of time where I'll be. America's Most Wanted and all that."

"Completely understandable," he said as I followed him out of the library and further down the hall. "I'm not sure if you are aware of the chaos Portland has been in the last five or six years, but we've taken a direct approach to establishing order in our fair city. It has become much safer for those who reside here."

"I've noticed a lot less of it being on the news channels. Haven't been in the area in a while though. I'm guessing there's less chaos, or the news would still be all over it. That's all they do."

"Not an overabundance of faith in our intrepid journalists?"

"Oh, I have all kinds of faith in them. I have complete faith that they'll do anything for a sound byte."

He chuckled. "I couldn't agree more. The lovely Virginia Madsen happens to be the hand behind the local puppet show."

"The one who *really* wanted to meet me?"

"One and the same. She has a particular skill with the use of pheromones. We call her the Romancer."

"Romancer?"

"Yes, of course. We are all ancers of some sort. I am a master of electric current, the Electromancer. Douglas, who you'll meet in a moment, can manipulate water in ways that would astound you."

"Aquamancer?"

He placed a finger to his nose with another smile that made me want to take a shower. I really didn't like Milo at first impression, and it wasn't getting better the longer I was in his presence.

We entered a room with a long table surrounded by lavish seats.

"Nice."

"Yes."

Four seats were occupied. A large blocky man with close-cut grey hair was in the first seat from the left of the head of the table. The chair was backed with blue velvet. Directly across from him sat a small-framed Latina woman. Her chair was red with orange highlights.

"I'm guessing, fire and water?"

"Correct. Douglas Gant, our Aquamancer, and Geneva Reyez, Pyromancer."

They nodded toward me in turn. Further down the table were two more on the right side, one in a silvery metal-hued velvet chair and the other in a black seat.

"I'm at a loss for these two," I said. "I get the idea with the green, brown, blue, and the one with the heart. Well maybe anyway."

"Black is my brother, Jared. He can speak to the dead."

"No shit? Necromancer?"

"The recently dead still have memories in their brains," Jared said. I can see them for a while after death.

"That's a new one on me," I said. "I've been around the better part of a century, and I've never seen that. I'm impressed."

The blonde necromancer smiled, and I was much less impressed with the air of arrogance he exuded.

"And our other Councilor is extremely good with technology," Milo said motioning toward the skinny guy with glasses who sat in the silvery chair. "Walter Kane is the Technomancer."

He nodded at me. "I am curious, Mister Lloyd, if you have someone of a similar persuasion who keeps things tidied up for you? When we thought of using you for this, I searched very deeply for you, but I hit walls. A lot of walls. Very good walls. There are, perhaps, seven people in the country who can do that, and we tend to stay out of each other's business. You may not wish to reveal your friend, but I wish to send a message to them. My hat is off to their skill. I am impressed."

"Thanks." I pointed at one of the chairs. "Will your Geomancer mind if I sit?"

"Not at all." Milo sat in the chair at the head of the table that had carved lightning bolts.

"So, tell me, what is it you need from me?"

"Sir, we would like for you to steal a rock."

"I'm guessing it isn't just any rock."

"And it's not just anywhere either," Milo said. "It's in a place you're intimately familiar with. A certain black site in Prescott, Arizona."

"Now I'm a little surprised. You do know that they're the very people who're the cause of all the turmoil in my life?"

"And we thought you'd jump at the chance to hurt them once more."

I remembered the hail of bullets that took my brother's life.

"You know? You're actually right. What's the pay? And what's so special about this rock?"

# Chapter 13

"Next!"

I stepped forward in the line for the food truck. "Let me get one of those loaded platters."

"Sure thing, honey." The lady in the truck said. "Do you want a to-go box with it?"

"I'll eat it here."

She looked at me with an eyebrow raised.

I smiled.

"Okay, honey. Don't say I didn't warn you. The truck is called Loaded for a reason."

I understood her skepticism. I was a five foot nothing "ninety five" pound woman with green hair. It seemed to fit right into the crowds in Portland.

I really still weighed close to two fifty. Part of the reason was the huge platter of food I was about to eat. I had to constantly fuel the body because the more mass I had to work with, the more variety I could use. Haley Curtis, my current identity, was small but everything in her makeup was twice as dense.

It was the first thing I did when I left the Elemental Club. I left the Escalade in the parking lot and walked away. I shifted seven times before settling into a premade alias.

The platter was huge and piled high with chicken, fish, slaw, and fries. It would probably make two meals for most people. While I devoured every crumb, I thought about what to do.

The "rock" was a solid chunk of *the* asteroid. Rumor was that they were experimenting on people with it. They'd had it in their possession for less than a month, but people were dying when they touched it. It was only safe to touch by a Talent.

I had a feeling they weren't telling me everything, but if a fraction of what they said was true, it needed to be removed from the base as quickly as possible.

I looked up as I ate the last fry to find several people staring at me, including the lady in the truck who nodded and grinned.

I smiled and waved before walking down the street. The only way to keep my mass high was to feed it. Once the food was eaten, I could use it with my Talent. I seemed to have plateaued at about two fifty. I guess the size was determined by my original body. At ninety-three, two hundred and fifty pounds was pretty big.

If I shifted into smaller people, I was stronger than a bigger person because of the density, but my greatest defense had always been the ability to make myself malleable. When I was young, I could create dense shields like when I was trying to get Adam out of the base. I didn't do that as much anymore. Took a lot of mass to build it.

I ducked into another store and went to the men's clothing where I took a few outfits from the racks to the cashier.

"Wow, these are all the same size I wear," he said.

"That's funny," I said. "What are the chances of that?"

We laughed and I paid for the clothes. I slipped out the door and into the one next door where I used the bathroom to shift and change. Then I walked out of the back door as the clerk from the other store. I was pretty sure I'd lost anyone trying to follow but I still shifted three more times before stopping to buy another prepaid phone.

Dialing in the number, I sat down on a bench.

"This better be good, I'm creating a masterpiece with this haircut."

"I'm guessing you're back in LA."

"What gave me away?"

"Heh, smart ass."

"What do you need?"

"I need to meet and talk in person. How hot is LA after the warehouse?"

"This place is crawling with suits."

"Shit. Frisco isn't any better."

"Get a room and call me from there. I'll come to you. Get me some clothes… and they better be nice. I'll close the shop after this one."

"Will do. Sorry, Kel. Be careful, they *do* have someone here like you said."

"Least I can do, asshole. And I'm always careful."

"Emperor Hijiro was forced to cancel his landing in Chicago this morning due to inclement weather conditions. Deadre LeMonte has offered to step in and fix the conditions if the city will allow it. Otherwise, the Emperor will continue on to Philadelphia…"

I'd met LeMonte back in '98. She was a weather witch. Manipulating the conditions that created weather was an art as much as it was a skill. She was in college learning how to use her talent to its potential. She also liked to get high and have sex in the weirdest places. On top of the weather tower surrounded by what seemed like living winds around us. Those were good times.

She was in her fifties and the picture on the television screen still brought back memories.

"Still looking good, Dee."

"Dee?" I turned to find Kelen had materialized next to the phone. He looked toward the screen. "You mean Deadre LeMonte or are you just commenting on my lovely self?"

"Definitely Deadre."

"Hmpf." He looked at the clothes waiting on the bed. "You brought me a suit?"

"You said get something nice."

"Honey." He motioned toward himself with both hands. "Can you even see the magnificence that is *this* in something like that?"

"It's either that or a bathrobe."

"Sometimes I wonder why I even fuckin' bother."

I chuckled. "You love me."

He pulled the black suit pants over his legs. "Love, hate, it's all so mixed up."

He threw the shirt aside and took the vest I had hanging on my headboard.

"That's min—"

His finger waggled at me as he slipped the green vest on. "I even make your awful suits look good. So, tell me how bad it is."

"You know about the thing in '58. What I did there after they killed Adam. Well, I need to go back to Prescott. They have something they can't be allowed to keep."

"They killing telepaths again?"

"Rumor is, they found a solid piece of the asteroid and they're testing it on people. It's killing folks and changing others. First, I need to know if it's true. Second, if it is, you have to get everything you can on the base because I'm gonna steal it."

"And what are these Talents going to do with it?"

"Probably not gonna give it to them either. I don't like them."

"Talents, in general? Or these in particular?"

"These in particular. I met five and they all had the same attitude. Like they were Lords and Ladies of royalty, maybe. Never liked that attitude and I've rarely found any with it that were inherently good. I don't hate every Talent."

"I'm so relieved you don't hate *all* Talents. I just don't know if I could live with that."

"Smart ass."

"Now it's time for you to buy dinner."

"You just banked sixteen million dollars."

"And?"

I chuckled and shifted into another woman with purple hair. "Fine."

"Since when have you been into the colored hair?"

"Have you been to Portland?"

He laughed.

"You don't have to change a thing, though. You fit right in."

"Town must be full of gorgeous people then."

I opened a duffle and pulled out clothes more suitable for the body I was wearing. Cut off shorts, halter top, panties, and a sports bra.

"They have some good food trucks. I know one that's supposed to have some great barbecue. Watched a show when I got the room about food trucks."

"You and your food trucks." He shook his head.

"They have some of the best food."

"I have to admit the one you took me to in LA had some of the best tacos."

"Carnitas," I said as I pulled the shorts over my hips. With just a few tweaks the body filled the shorts perfectly.

"You don't even have to shop for sizes," he said. "Sometimes I hate you."

"I'll try to live with the guilt," I said as my boobs grew to fill the top to almost overflowing.

"Asshole."

"Let's go get some barbecue," I said.

"Ten dollars says you'll drop something down your shirt with those sticking out that far."

"I don't drop food in my boobs."

He shook his head again before opening the door and stepping out.

"The way you were talking about LeMonte back there sounded like you knew her. You didn't sleep with her, too, did you?"

"Maybe a couple of times. Dangerous to sleep with a weather witch. Might get struck by lightning or something else equally crazy."

"Sweetie, *you* need supervision."

# Chapter 14

Three hours later, after I paid Kelen his ten dollars and cleaned the sauce from where it fell, we bought a pickup truck in the name of Liza Dorn, my current identity. An hour out of Portland, Kelen dove into the computer on the truck and used its Wi-Fi to return to LA where he would dig for information. I was driving southeast on I-84 where I would go through Idaho and down through Utah.

I planned to stop in Salt Lake City and wait for Kelen to return. I didn't want to go into the base blind, and I was sure they'd changed things since my last visit. I knew some people in Salt Lake and figured I could check up on them while I was in town.

In the '90s there had been a lot of comic book style super heroes. Talents had embraced the whole hero/villain thing. That's where I met Fire and Ice. They were siblings and I used to have a thing with Ice. He was a little put out when he found out I was a shifter and had just spent the better part of a year as one of his girlfriends, he had several. He never got past the fact my original form was male, so we broke up. It was thirty years ago, and I figured he was probably over that by now.

Hell, I lived through the '60s, it was free love for everyone. I guess I was kind of equal opportunity when it came to that, although I enjoyed women a little more these days, preferably BENT. I didn't have to hide as much from the BENT. They see that I can shift, and it doesn't freak them out. When Twilight saw my true form, I was surprised when she decided to stay as long as she did and even more surprised when she asked me to go with her. A fat naked ninety three year old is probably not the most appealing sight.

It was getting late, so I pulled into a small hotel and got a room. I probably should have shifted from the shape of Liza Dorn before doing so but I'm not certain it would make a difference in what happened.

I was sitting on the bed wearing yoga pants and the sport bra, shifting into several people I was trying to remember correctly when I noticed something. I wouldn't have noticed except one of the shifts had let my eyes run through several spectrums as they changed. They caught an odd glow.

I stood up and pulled the cover from a vent duct. Inside was a camera and the wire ran to a small box with an antenna.

"Fuck." A sinking feeling ran through my chest. "Perv."

There was no guarantee whoever was on that other end was any more than someone getting their jollies watching cute girls in the rooms, but I am America's Most Wanted. I couldn't take the chance.

I dialed Kel, leaving a message. "May be burnt. You may want to clean the truck, can't take it with me. I'll get back in touch."

Then I took some lipstick from my bag and wrote on the wall under the vent. "Might want to look for cameras. Perv alert!"

Taking out the small bag that held my phone, cards, and IDs, I stripped and shifted. Smaller and smaller I shrank. Going small wasn't as easy as shifting same sizes. Your muscles are denser, bones are denser, everything is. With the same mass in a small package, you are stronger than you have any right to be. I picked up the six inch hand bag and looped the straps over my shoulders like a giant backpack. I was about two inches taller than the bag. I flipped a bird at the camera and kicked a hole in the wall at the back of the unit.

"Stupid asshole," I muttered. "I aught to crawl up his ass and expand to full size." That was a disturbing thought. "Yuk."

It only took a few moments until I was standing outside the rear of the building in front of an eight inch hole.

"Hope a raccoon moves in."

Turning toward the woods behind the hotel, I leapt about ten feet. Then I did it again. When I reached the woods, I dropped the bag and shifted into a wolf. I picked up the bag in my teeth and loped deeper into the woods. There was a mountain and I climbed to an outcropping where I could observe the hotel.

I was impressed with the response time of the local Feds. They were there in under two hours from the time I found the camera. I'd been there for a couple of hours already, but I had no idea when the guy actually called. Everybody wants the ten million bucks on my head. Hopefully he'd get his ass in jail for spying on his guests.

The first two SUVs stopped just outside of the hotel and six agents exited each one to start spreading around the hotel.

"Too late," I said as I shifted back to human. I pulled the phone and called Kel.

"What exactly the hell is wrong with you? No sightings in ten years and now three incidents in the last two months."

"I guess luck caught up. It's a definite burn though. Feebs just surrounded the place."

"Are you inside?"

"No. I'm old, not slow."

"Old and slow if you're still where you can see it."

"Figured I'd make sure. I like the truck."

"Get out of there and I'll burn any link."

"Gotcha." I started sprouting wings. "Nearest safe house would be Mountain Home?"

"Yes, if you still plan to go to Salt Lake."

"I should have just gone on through Boise and stopped there anyway."

"Or you could quit shifting in public."

"In my defense it was because the guy was spying on his guests."

"Scan for that shit!"

"You do have a little advantage in that department."

"Then buy a damn scanner. For the life of me, I don't even know how you survived fifty years without me."

"Heh."

"That's right. Now get your ass to the safe house."

"I'm flying out now, see ya soon." I said and hung up. My wings were done so I jumped off of the cliff with my bag in hand.

The horizon was just beginning to light up when I dropped into the back yard of the cabin in Mountain Home, Idaho.

"Good thing it didn't take longer," I muttered. "Naked women with wings would spark questions."

# Chapter 15

I'd owned the cabin for close to sixty years. It was the first place I bought after I began to work with Jasper. He was an Illusionist and petty criminal. He kept me from becoming what the government claimed I was. We'd spent a lot of years hiding in places like this. Hiding in plain sight. The Cabin was away from the road and surrounded by flat scrubland. When I looked out the front door, I could see a subdivision in the distance that wasn't there last time I was here. I was still the end of the lane and mostly had scrub around my place.

"Places have a tendency to grow when you aren't looking," I said to myself.

I remembered sitting at the dining table behind me plotting heists or con jobs with Jasper. He always made the plans and kept the jobs free of violence. It gave me time to put a damper on the rage that filled me in those days. I didn't feel that rage so much anymore. Sometimes I was just tired.

So, I stood looking out my front door drinking coffee and wondering what the hell I was doing wrong. It all started going south when I tangled with that Talent. They got a bead on me again and now they were looking for the bogey man behind every stone. If I could trust the powers that be with the rock, I would just walk away.

But the story Milo had told me was all too believable after seeing those telepaths lobotomized. If they could do that, they wouldn't hesitate to test something like this on people whether it was killing them or not.

Over the next few days, I got Kelly Price down the best I could remember and then aged her thirty years. Fire and Ice both knew I was a shapeshifter but anyone who saw an old flame show up thirty years later needed to see thirty years. She was still pretty attractive, I'd modeled Sophia in New York from the same mold. Kelly Price was beautiful back then and thirty years later wasn't much less attractive, just older. I'd seen many people who aged well over the years, and I had to give them the credit they were due.

My original body was not the best to gauge that sort of thing. I hadn't gone back to that except the one time, and I didn't plan to do that again.

"Not tangling with Talents," I said and blew on my coffee to cool it.

I was surprised it was taking Kelen so long to do a deep dive of Prescott, but it would stand to reason the government would be using top of the line defenses for their computers. I'd never seen anything top of the line enough to stop him though.

Since I was pretty sure my Kelly Price persona was pretty good, I shifted into Sophia Ritten whose ID was still safe since she was a loner who didn't show up on anything related to the New York thing except a search into her background done by the Kazaskis who were gone.

My ID should still be clean enough to buy a car.

I called an Uber to give me a ride to Jack Hedder Chevrolet where I purchased a two year old Suburban. I liked the big SUVs, and the Suburban was one of the biggest out there. The size let me be any one of my IDs comfortably. Although I didn't see shifting into a dude any time soon with the outfit I was wearing. I could probably get away with it in Portland but not Salt Lake.

I was actually looking forward to seeing the twins. Time had just flown by since I left there in '92. How did I go this long without going back? I guess the thing in 2000 caused that. I was basically underground for ten years after that.

I got outed by some people I had done some work for. I was careless for just a moment, and someone saw dollar signs. Needless to say, I wouldn't be going to Florida again in the next twenty years. They fielded more agents than you could shake a stick at when they got the report. I barely got out of that mess intact. Ended up swimming up the coast to Brunswick, Georgia as a shark. I was pretty happy I had studied those two years in Marine Biology when I was at the University with Deadre. I even had functioning gills.

That particular skill had come in quite handy over the years. I wondered if I could actually study the designs of a scanner for wires like Kelen was talking about and form one that worked. Maybe I would look into it when this caper was over. Sometimes technology kept advancing so fast I couldn't keep up. Or I just got complacent, which could very well be.

I'd studied metallurgy some when designing the finger blades and spent four years in med school learning about human biology, so I didn't turn into something that killed me.

There was a size shifter back in the '70s that was pretty popular. He'd shrink and do super strength stuff. He tried to go giant one time and his body was dispersed too far by the air flows to come back together. His loss was a lesson to a lot of us shifters. Stay within your mass parameters. I'd never met any shifter that wasn't under the constraint of mass.

That's why I ate so much. More mass available. It's also why I spent as much time as I did as a woman. Smaller frame meant denser structure and gave me a huge advantage in strength. I'd been closer to three hundred pounds twenty years back. Age, I presumed took its toll. I had to eat a large amount of food just to maintain two fifty these days.

It was only a couple of hundred miles down to Salt Lake from Mountain Home and I drove at a leisurely pace. I wondered how hard it would be to find the twins. They were pretty famous in the day. I'd find out when I got to the city. I could use a library computer to look them up if Kelen hadn't returned by then.

"I'm old, not useless," I muttered under my breath.

# Chapter 16

I pulled the Suburban into a drive where a Lincoln crossover was already sitting. The internet, if I wasn't completely useless, said this is where Diane Richie, aka Fire, lived. I had intended to see Ice first but there wasn't anything about him, which worried me a bit.

I rang the doorbell and waited.

The door opened and an older version of Diane was staring at me. She was still pretty but age had taken the young firecracker I used to know. It only took a few moments for her eyes to glow before she clamped down on the anger that caused it.

"Guess you're still mad," I said.

"Mad?" Her eyes narrowed. "Where the hell have you been? You disappeared."

"I thought it was made pretty clear I wasn't welcome."

She took a deep breath and let it out slowly. Then she shook her head. "Come in, Kelly. Or whoever you really are."

I grimaced. "Are you sure?"

"Yes, I'm sure. I wouldn't invite you in if I wasn't."

"Still pretty straight forward."

"I don't have time for making a bunch of shit up. Don't even know how you do that."

"I don't have any choice."

"That's what you said before you disappeared the last time. There's always a choice."

"Sometimes the choice is made a long time ago and there's not a lot to be done about it."

"He never got over you." She pointed toward a chair.

I sat and looked around at the place. The walls were in a light blue and pictures hung in different patterns. Most of them were of the two of them. Fire was short and slim with a huge mane of blonde hair where Ice was six feet tall and built like an athlete. His blonde hair was the same color as hers, but he kept it cropped close.

"That's hard to believe," I said. "I was just one of many."

She pointed at one of the pictures with a young Kelly Price being carried in the arms of Garrett Richie. Ice was looking down at her with a smile on his face. "He lost that smile when you disappeared."

"He wouldn't even look at me after I told him what I was."

"He would have gotten over it if you'd stayed."

"Maybe," I said. "I couldn't stay anyway. It was a pipe dream to even think I could."

"Why? Why couldn't you?"

"There are reasons I can't stay anywhere long. I thought I could swing by and just spend a day with some old friends. I guess that might be a pipe dream too. I can't find much on Garrett so I thought I might see if you would tell me where I can find him. Obviously, there's a lot of anger still here. Maybe I should go."

I stood up to leave.

"No. You aren't going to find him right now. He's in an institute designed for Talents with ailments."

"What?"

"A few years ago, he started losing control of his powers. The doctors discovered the onset of Alzheimer's. It's gotten worse since then. He lives in the past and he's not getting any better. Part of why I'm so angry with you is that you are one of the only things he remembers."

I sighed. "That's just not fair. I'm sorry, if that means anything."

"What was it that was so important you had to disappear for thirty years?"

"Kel's gonna kill me." I took a deep breath and let it out slowly. "Have you been watching the news?"

"Off and on."

"You see about the thing in New York with the feds? Then later in LA?"

"The ones about that… Holy shit!"

"Yeah."

"You're *that* shapeshifter?"

"Yeah. I can't stay anywhere. The fact that I just told you means I have to go. It's the only way I've stayed ahead of them. They've been hounding me for over sixty years. Sometimes I get to rest somewhere like I did here. I was younger and still thought I could settle somewhere."

"Why can't you?"

"Age."

"What do you mean?"

"These are things I should have said before I left. Some of it I didn't even know yet, I guess. I understand what's happening. I don't have the control I used to either. It's harder to do what I do. The thing in New York should never have happened. You've fought Talents back when you were doing the hero thing. It's hard to do and it takes a lot out of you. This time it took too much, and I lost all of it. I was laying there unconscious in my original form and helpless."

"Jesus."

"Twilight saved my life when she carried me out of there. Feds were all over that place in less than an hour. I have no doubts what they would have done."

"But they didn't."

"Yeah, because of her."

"They say you freed a lot of women and shut down a human trafficking ring."

"The news doesn't usually say anything about that part."

"No, they don't." She smiled. "But there's a lot that gets passed around behind the scenes from Talents and BENT alike. There were a lot of BENT that live there that saw what happened. They saw family returned to them and they spread the word. They saw a crime lord and his little empire completely destroyed. Heroes still exist."

"I'm no hero."

"I beg to differ. Sean Halleck, aka Dragon scale, fought numerous heroes in the late 2000s and went underground when the government started getting involved. He was a very bad guy and a strong Talent. You killed him in a warehouse where he held close to forty women in chains. That's straight up hero shit."

"Dragon scale. I knew he looked familiar."

She pointed toward the chair again. "I can't report you if you're still sitting here. Sit, just sit and talk for a bit."

I returned to the chair.

"I want you to know he doesn't have much longer. They're saying it's days or weeks, not months. I know you don't feel like you can trust anyone, but I'd like to ask for a favor. I need you to do something for me."

"I wouldn't have told you if I didn't trust you. That year was one of the best years of my life. I had a family again for a while."

Two hours later, I walked into a room in the Janasecki Institute.

"Kelly?"

I sat on the bed beside him as he talked to me just like it was yesterday. The next day it was a repeat of the first, and I did it again every day for the next ten days. I held his hand at the end, and I drove south out of Salt Lake with tears streaming down my face.

# Chapter 17

I rented another room at a motel just before the Nevada line. I remembered this one from a few years ago. I ran the new gadget I had bought at an electronics store over the room. It was designed to detect any transmissions from cameras or mikes. Then did a visual inspection as well.

Afterwards, I went back out to the Suburban and brought in several bags. There were five bottles of various kinds of rum and five bottles of different brands of Scotch. Garrett loved Scotch. I lined them up along the dresser in front of the TV hanging on the wall.

I opened the Glenlivet thirty year Scotch. I figured I should start with the good one. At thirteen hundred dollars a bottle, it better be good. And I sure didn't want to waste it by drinking it after I was so drunk, I couldn't tell the difference.

My phone rang. I picked it up and the room flashed as Kelen materialized in front of me.

"You look like shit." He walked to the bathroom and grabbed a robe from the closet. "Honey, have you been crying?"

"Maybe."

He looked at the line of bottles. "Tell me."

Afterwards he reached toward me. "Give me a bottle, too. It looks like we gonna be drinking for a while. The rest of this can wait."

We drank… a lot.

"Are you okay?"

I pulled the shirt on and buttoned it. "Yeah, I'm alright."

"I'm not," Kelen said holding his head. "I hate you right now. You don't have the least bit of a hangover?"

"Don't really have those anymore."

"Bastard. Give me your phone."

I handed him the cell phone and he flashed and disappeared. The phone fell to the bed before it flashed again, and he was back.

"Better?"

"Damn straight. You're not the only one with talent."

"Yeah, we can drink ten bottles of hooch and survive it."

"Looked like you were planning to drink ten by yourself."

"I was thinking about it."

"I know it took a while, but I found a lot of information once I got past their defenses. They have a talented cyber guy. I still got away with a lot of video files you'll want to see."

"You need me to go get a laptop?"

"This'll do, sweetie, it's not the computer that does this." He touched the side of the TV and his eyes flashed in rapid succession. "This is the first one they tried."

The image was of an old man who looked like he was probably from the streets.

"I get a hundred bucks to touch a rock?"

"Absolutely." The voice came from somewhere off screen. "Just touch it and the money's yours."

The old man touched a reddish colored rock and screamed as his arm turned black. Not like it was burned but like obsidian stone. He stopped screaming as the stone reached about halfway across his body.

"Then it's true," the voice said. "A touch can change anyone."

"It may just kill anyone, sir."

"Guess we'll have to test further."

"That sounds about like the guys that used to run the place," I said. "They don't care about the body count."

"I can attest to that. I watched every one of the videos. It changes anyone who touches it, but it kills them because it's too potent. They killed fifty people before they tried it on someone BENT."

"Shit."

"Yep."

The scene shifted to a young man with feathers for hair who stood before the camera.

"All you have to do is touch the rock and you'll get the cash."

"Aw, don't touch it," I said.

He touched the rock, and he staggered as the shirt swelled and ripped when wings sprouted from his back. You could see the muscles shifting in his back as they adapted to the new appendages. The wings spread wide as he screamed. It took a few minutes before he dropped to his knees and huddled inside the multicolored wings. When he turned back toward the camera, his eyes were much larger and golden hued. He was beautiful.

"Interesting." The voice from off camera was cold. "Pay it."

I didn't like the way he said that at all.

Gas flooded the chamber and the bird man thrashed inside of the chamber hard enough to put a hairline crack in the thick glass.

"They have to be stopped," I said as the man struggled to breath.

"Damn right they do." Kelen took his hand from the TV. "They've done this to seven people who were BENT. Each one has been changed into near Talent levels. Some, like that one would be considered a Talent if he had been permitted to live."

"I sense a 'but' coming."

"Honey, they have defenses designed specifically for you. During the thing in '58, they managed to get some of your DNA. That's something that stays the same whether you're shifted or not. That's how they confirmed it was you in New York. You were in your natural form and left hair behind. When you're shifted you don't lose hair like the rest of us."

"I get that."

"But they've been working on machines to detect particular DNA and this place is where it started. Every floor has scanners that are always on. Every door has them installed. You step through one of those and it sets off alarms throughout the whole place."

"You can't do something with those?"

"Sweetie, I'm good. I may be the best out there, but they have at least three Talents of a similar persuasion working that base. I can take the scanners out, but they'd catch it in seconds. Those scanners going down would mean only one thing because they're designed for *you* and you alone. They're scared."

"Why would they think I'm coming back? It's been sixty years."

"You must have left quite the impression."

"Yeah, I guess I did."

It was a lot easier to control my abilities when I was younger, lightning fast adaptations as I waded through the agents kept them unable to target me. If they got near me, they went down. Bullets went through me like water and hit others behind me.

"I don't think I could do that again," I said. "I have to put a lot more effort into the changes."

"Plus, they have agents that are Talents."

"Fuck."

"You can say that again. One of them is Frank Steiner."

"Steiner? I hate that guy."

"Everyone hates Steiner. I don't understand how he's not in prison."

"Look who he's working for. They aren't known for playing by the rules. I doubt they worried about what he did in '08."

"I don't think I like the CIA."

"I already knew I didn't like them." I sat down in the chair and stared at the TV. "I might have an idea about getting around most of that. How thick are the walls around the facility underground?"

"You'd have to dig eight levels down to reach the room where the rock is kept, then go through three feet of concrete and steel."

"I know a guy."

"Of course, you know a guy."

"Problem is he's almost as old as I am and the other one's just as old." I tapped my fingers on the arm of the chair. "She could do the concrete and steel."

"What does she do to concrete and steel?" he asked.

"She eats it," I said. "At least the parts of it that matter."

"Where are they?"

"Where do you think they are? New York."

"The last place you were actually seen. Of course, that's where they are."

"At least they're just in upstate New York and not in the city. They don't keep retired Talents inside the city."

"You mean they're in Red Hook?"

"They were six years ago. If we go by the last month, they probably already died. I'm two for two at the moment."

Kel placed a hand on my shoulder and squeezed.

# Chapter 18

I jumped as Kelen materialized right in front of me on the plane.

"That was close," he said. "You gotta time a plane jump perfectly."

I shook my head. "You could have called first and warned me. What if I'd been having some fun time with a stewardess?"

"They're called flight attendants now, fossil. And last time I looked you don't have any on this plane."

"Always just showing up out of thin air…"

"What were you doing?"

"Nothing."

"Then what are you bitching about. I don't fuss when you show up out of the blue—"

"Bullshit. You start whining when I step in the door and don't stop until I leave."

He started laughing. "You may be right. Where're my clothes?"

I motioned toward the back of the cabin with my thumb.

"Hmpft."

I grinned as he headed to the back. We'd gotten over nakedness a long time ago. Both of our Bends didn't include clothing and after nearly a hundred years, I'd seen pretty much everything.

After a few minutes, he exited the cabin wearing a pair of silver yoga pants and a fuchsia tank top.

Well, almost everything. "Jesus, it gets worse every time."

"You can just shut your cake hole. Do you realize your 'crew' has a cumulative age of more than three centuries?"

"Yeah, I guess so. I can't even believe they're both still alive. I hope they're up to it."

"Me too, we're breaking into one of the most secure facilities in the country."

"Just secure from me," I said. "They don't have DNA scanners for anyone but me, do they?"

"They do. It's not all about *you*, America's MWP."

"I like to think of it as MVP."

"If you count the bounty, you may be right. It seems like you keep sticking your head up every twenty years or so and it climbs. Did you know they raised it to fifteen after that SNAFU in New York?"

"It's been ten since 2000. I wonder why they upped it."

"Because they found solid evidence, you're still out there causing problems."

"Fixing problems," I muttered.

"Ten bodies and a Talent this time."

"If that bastard wasn't so tough, I could have cleaned the scene properly."

"Instead, you left a bunch of DNA and had to be saved by a girl."

"True enough."

"You understand we need to check your background before letting you interview them?" The young man seemed quite apologetic.

"Absolutely," I said. "It's a secure facility."

"It'll only take a few minutes Miss Darby."

"I'll wait." I sat in one of the comfortable lobby seats. "These are nice."

"What's nice?" Kel's voice asked in my ear. I'd taken the earbud and pulled it inside my ear and out of sight. His voice was still clear.

"The chairs in the lobby."

I heard a sigh.

"What?"

"Nothing. Quit talking to yourself in the lobby. You look like a crazy lady."

I chuckled.

"Now you're laughing at the voices in your head. How the hell have you managed not to get caught?"

"I usually work alone," I muttered. "Without some asshole in my ear."

Kelen laughed. "Guy's coming back."

I stopped acting like a crazy lady since there was now an audience. Instead, I crossed my right leg over my left, letting the skirt slide up a little.

"Really?" Kelen asked.

I kept my eyes lowered as I read the newspaper I had picked up.

"Quit trying to line up the next bit of fluff and listen. Your guy Higgins is in the basement. They let him use the underground parts of the facility with his preference for underground environs."

"Underground environs?" I asked behind the newspaper.

"Their words, not mine."

I let the paper drop for an instant to find the young man behind the desk staring at my legs. His eyes turned quickly, and his face turned red.

"You just can't help yourself." Kelen said.

"What fun is it to be a shapeshifter if you can't play with it," I whispered.

He sighed again and I grinned.

"Uh…ma'am, the check cleared. You can do your interviews."

I stood up and turned to lay the paper on the table beside the chair.

"Oh my God. Stop torturing that boy."

"Thank you, sir," I said as I returned to the desk where his face was still a little red.

"Doctor Feige will be down to escort you inside. There are certain places you won't be allowed to go. Some of these people are dangerous."

"Old timers can be cranky."

"Add a Bend or talent to the mix and they can be pretty volatile," he said. "I'm certainly glad to be working the front desk."

"Sounds like you don't like them very much."

"Sometimes I wonder if they wouldn't be better off without it."

"Don't we all?" I mused.

A short black woman in a white frock opened a door to our left.

"Miss Darby?"

I nodded and followed her back into the facility after giving the young man at the desk a smile I was sure he wouldn't forget.

"I understand you wish to interview some of the guests?"

"Yes," I said. "I'm doing an article on my blog about retirement for those with talents and how they adjust."

"It sounds interesting," she said. "You can talk with almost any of our guests if they agree. There are some on the upper floors that are just too dangerous. Uncontrolled Talents are a frightening thing. Some of them just lose too much control and have to be kept isolated. This is the biggest reason they come to Red Hook in the first place. They know we can help keep them from hurting people.

"Many of the staff have their own talents and it helps the others to realize we are here for them."

"Very interesting," I said. "What sort of talents do you find beneficial in your staff?"

"Strength is always helpful. Those with enhanced strength tend to be heavier than your normal person. But there are many talents that are useful. Even some of the younger guests have joined the staff when they've needed a hand. We like to be considered a family of sorts."

"That's great. I want to focus the article on how well the guests are treated and that is exactly the kind of thing I need."

"Excellent. Is there anywhere in particular you'd like to start?"

"Wherever you think would be a wise place to begin is fine. I would love to talk to everyone, but we'll see how many I can interview today."

"Of course."

Annoyed with Lloyd

# Chapter 19

The interviews continued for several hours before the doctor left me alone with the guests. I went straight to room 345 once she left. I had been bouncing around randomly for the first few hours just so it wouldn't look suspicious when I got the opportunity.

I knocked on the door.

When it opened, I almost didn't recognize Cynthia. It had been close to twenty years since I had visited, and I expected her to have aged, but this was excessive.

"You're that reporter?"

"Yes."

"Not interested."

"Not even for an old friend?" I shifted my face after making sure there were no cameras.

Her jaw dropped. "Jesus Christ, what are you doing here?"

"Thought you and Sam might be interested in doing a job."

She sighed. "Can't you just get someone a little younger?" She pulled me into the room. "Oh, come in. I have to say you picked a pretty skin suit. But I guess you were always good at that."

"You *do* put more thought into the women you shift into," Kelen said in my ear.

"Speaking of youngsters, I do have one with me." I tapped my ear.

"Do I have to be careful what I say?"

I shook my head. "He's safe."

"Normally, I'd need to meet them but if he hasn't turned you in for the fifteen million…"

"I see you've been watching the news."

"Sam and I have been keeping up. You really screwed the pooch in New York City. How'd you manage to get caught in your original body there?"

"Can't do what I used to, anymore."

"None of us can. That's why we're here. Where will you go when you can't keep it under control?"

"I don't know, Cyn. This place seems nice though."

"It has ties to the government. You'd never get to stay here. If you were a year later, they'd have some new scanners they've been talking about."

"DNA scanners?"

"You've heard of them?"

"Yeah, we're familiar. A place like this I could probably still get into. They don't have the techs that the target has."

"This target's government?"

"CIA black site."

"You don't have a very good history with those."

"This one in particular."

"You want to go back there? What's the matter with you?"

"Can you show her, Kel?"

The TV came to life, and she looked at me with an eyebrow raised.

"He's good with computers."

"Good with computers? Honey, I should leave right now."

I chuckled and pointed at my ear. "Getting chewed out." I pointed at the screen. "They found a solid chunk of the asteroid and they're experimenting on people."

We watched what they did to the BENT after the normal and the single time they used a Talent. He was a soldier who could teleport about ten feet ahead of himself.

"I don't want to touch that," he said.

The same guy we had watched eliminate anyone who survived answered, "You know who we are and the trouble we can cause for you and your family. Your mother is living quite well in Chicago. I'd hate to see something happen…"

"You people are some real bastards. I did two tours in the desert for this country."

"And now you'll do another brave thing for your country."

He sighed and touched the rock. Then he vanished.

"Where did he go? He's not supposed to be able to teleport unless he can see where he's going!"

"Sir, there's nowhere he could see except that room."

The video ended.

"They would have killed that boy too, wouldn't they?" she asked.

"No guarantees, but you saw the same thing I have. They can't keep it, the people that hired me can't have it, and I can't get to it without help."

"And what do you need 'Glow' for?"

"I need 'Digger' to get me eight stories below the ground and 'Glow' to weaken that concrete and steel enough for me to get into that room. We go in and snatch the rock, then hide it somewhere safe."

She sighed. "Retirement has been really nice, Alex."

"I know I don't have any right to ask it…"

"Bullshit. It's a moot point anyway. I've seen the videos and they can't keep it. Who wants to spend their last year in this place anyway?"

"Last year?"

"Oh, your tech guy didn't dig deep enough. I've got some nasty shit from using the glow so much. That's why I'm here. I'm sixty-two and look eighty."

"You're dying?"

"I am."

"I'll find another—"

"Alex, hush. I've been staring down the barrel of this for a while. I can help do something good before then."

"Damn it, Cyn."

"Now you better get out of here before you screw up and say something to the wrong person. Fifteen million would make it a damn fine year. I'll bring Sam. I might even bring Pender."

"Pender? Willy Pender is here?"

"He's been here a few months."

"You know he's bat shit crazy, right?"

"Yeah, but he lives for this kind of thing. Conspiracies are all over the place. He almost left after he found out Red Hook has ties to the government. He's crazy, but the bastard's a heavy hitter. Even at his age he can bench press a truck. He's a good backup if I can't do my thing."

I stood up with a hollow feeling in my chest. "We're at Falder's Airfield."

"We'll be there."

# Chapter 20

I didn't even flirt with the guy in the lobby as I went out. Cynthia had sent me into a spiral with her news of what I assumed was a cancer of some sort. I hadn't asked Kelen, and he was quiet as I left Red Hook.

That would be another of the few who knew me for who I was. The list shrank every day it seemed. Was I kidding myself about this job? They had Steiner inside that facility. Frank Steiner was a Talent with super strength and damn nigh indestructible. He was imprisoned for multiple murders and should have been in the Crypt, the prison in Olida for guys like him. If he got involved before we could get out of there, I wasn't sure I could do what I did with Halleck. Even if I could, I would be left in the worst place I could think of with nothing left.

But I couldn't let them keep doing what they were doing. They were doing the same kind of shit as the last time, and it had to stop. The plan was to do it quietly and they wouldn't even know until we were long gone.

"Emperor Hijiro's flight into New York is underway and all flights are canceled for the next three hours…" I changed the station.

"…latest Blue Tube challenge turned to tragedy again today as four local teens leapt from the Empire State building…" I turned the station again.

"Frigging idiots."

"…Darkness is interviewing for another apprentice after the latest protégé's untimely disappearance last year. After Timothy Darfis was found last month, Darkness announced that Darfis was indeed his erstwhile partner, Shade, and…" I turned the radio off.

"What the hell's wrong with the world?"

"That's a dumb assed question," Kelen said as he materialized in the passenger seat.

"How'd you do that when I turned it off?"

"Honey, I don't think you have any idea what I do. Where're my clothes?"

"Back seat."

"Oh hell, no. You did not bring me flannel. I told you something red."

"It's got red in it."

Kelen was grinding his teeth as he pulled the jeans and flannel shirt from the back seat.

"I refuse." He threw them in the back. "I'll be on the plane. Have a nice walk."

He glowed and flashed into the car's electronics which smelled funny for a second and the car shut off.

I chuckled as I let the car coast to the side of the road. "I probably deserved that."

Stepping out of the car, I flagged down the first vehicle that saw me. Elena Darby wasn't someone that would walk far before she would be picked up. It was a bit of a lottery-type situation after that. Apparently, my luck was going alright when I saw it was a woman. Well, possibly alright anyway.

A woman usually picks a woman up if she is worried something bad could happen to her if she doesn't. There are some that do it for nefarious purposes and when they're bad, they're worse than most men. Men are looking at a beautiful woman and want to be a hero or a villain. I found Alfiona Markus to be the first type.

"Girl, you have to be careful out here on the roads," the middle-aged black woman said. "There's all sorts of bad people out here."

"I know," I said. "Thank God you stopped."

She was quite nice and a pleasant relief to the caliber of people I usually ran into. I was at the airfield in less than thirty minutes and waved as Alfiona drove back down the road the way we came.

Kel sat on the stairs laughing.

"That was mean, man. Just mean."

"Flannel?"

"If you bothered to look a little deeper, you'd have seen the Louis Vuitton stuff in the floorboard."

"What?"

"Remember those red pants you were looking at back in LA?"

"You didn't."

"I did. But you automatically think the worst of me."

"Where are they?"

"Still where I left them unless the car's already been stripped."

"You left them in the car?"

"Yup." I walked past him into the plane.

"That's why I think the worst of you. You're an evil person, Alex."

I shrugged, sat down in one of the comfortable seats, and closed my eyes.

"Was there really a Louis Vuitton?"

"Go look."

"You know it would be worse. I can't carry anything."

"I know. Right?"

"You're a bastard."

"And then some."

"Shit…" He started to glow

Two and a half hours later he walked back on the plane wearing the shiny red pants and jacket that had been in the box I left in the car.

"It's not really fair that you get a ride so quick."

"If you wore the Armani, you'd have gotten a ride too."

"What's wrong with this?" He posed.

"A six-foot-tall blackish fella with a shiny red suit?"

"Blackish?"

I shrugged.

He stood there for a few minutes and looked down at the three thousand dollar pantsuit. Then he stepped forward and hugged me.

I chuckled as he walked to the back cabin.

"You're welcome, kid," I said softly.

# Chapter 21

"If what Cyn tells me is true, I'll do my best to help." Samuel 'Digger' Higgins said. He was rail thin but seemed otherwise healthy for a seventy-six-year-old man. "Not sure what you need a couple of old goats for, though. I know they're a lot younger Talents out there."

"Talents I can trust?"

"That would depend on you. Have you been nice, or have you been the asshole we all know?"

Kelen snorted.

Digger's eye was twitching as he looked at Kelen who wore yellow and white striped pants and a silver shirt. His short-cropped hair was done in a leopard pattern.

"Of course, I've been nice," I said.

"Sure, you have. I heard about something about a month and a half ago just across the other end of the state."

"Well now, that was a fluke."

"Ten dead bodies including Dragon scale."

"Respect," Willy Pender said. "He was strong."

"About did me in," I said, looking at Pender. He was still pretty big, even at seventy years old. Last time I saw him he had black hair and a bushy black beard. They both were white as snow now and a lot of his size was his frame.

"Glow tells me this thing you need to get is in a CIA black site. I've been telling people all along they need to keep an eye on those CIA bastards. It's a wonder they aren't all over us already."

"The CIA doesn't run Red Hook, Willy," Cynthia said. "But they may be trying to get their hooks in. That new security system they've been talking about adding sounds a lot like this place we're going."

"I told you."

"This doesn't have anything to do with Red Hook, though." She nodded toward Kel. "Can you show them what you showed me?"

Kel turned the screen on the swivel arm at the front of the cabin toward us and his eyes glowed.

"These first ones were regular people and it killed them outright," I said. "As you can see, they went through close to fifty people before they moved up to people with Bends. Six of those and you see the pattern. It makes the BENT into a Talent or it just amplifies that Bend to a very high degree. The latest was a soldier with a talent. They called him Blink. He could teleport to a spot in front of him that he could see."

They watched as the man who touched the rock vanished. "I'm not sure how they expected any other outcome. Amplify a talent for teleporting short distances and you probably have a long-distance teleporter. I hope he didn't teleport straight forward some huge distance or he'd be above falling since the world is round. Even worse if he went so far as to leave the atmosphere. The bottom line is that I can't allow people who would kill close to sixty people to see what it would do to keep the rock."

"Agreed," Digger said. "But how are you getting in there with the security measures Cyn mentioned?"

I nodded at Kelen, and the screen changed to a city map. "I want to start here."

I pointed at a warehouse two blocks from the one over the base. "We're gonna have to tunnel."

"I haven't dug anything like that in years," he said. "I'm not even sure I can do it now."

"If you can't, we'll have to come up with another plan," I said. "This is the only way I figure we can do this without setting off all sorts of alarms and they have Frank Steiner in there working with them."

"Jesus! Steiner?"

"I could slow down a guy like Steiner, but I don't think I could take him," Pender said. "The man is a beast."

"Thing is, if we do this right, they shouldn't even know it's gone until we're long gone."

"But I'll need to dig eight stories down and two blocks."

I nodded. "If you can get us to the wall, Cyn can weaken it enough for me to go through it and grab the stone. Then you collapse the tunnel after we're back out."

He chuckled.

"What?" I asked.

"Just like that time in Venus Beach."

"Pretty much."

"I don't know if I've got it in me, but I'll try. Venus Beach was sand and it's a lot easier to work with."

"You should've killed all those bastards the last time," Pender said.

"I did."

"Looks like they retrained a whole new generation of evil. Maybe they need to be cleaned out a little more frequently than sixty years apart."

"As much as I want to clear them out again, I'm nowhere near as spry as I was then. I hope we can get in and out without even being seen."

"Wish in one hand and shit in the other." Pender shrugged. "We'll see which fills up first."

"Speaking of shitting in one hand," Digger said. "I'll be right back." He stood and walked to the back.

"You think we can get in there without getting caught?"

"Willy, I expect to get seen as soon as we get to the city. Hope for the best but expect the worst."

"I guess if you expect the worst, you're never disappointed."

"True enough," I said with a grin.

# Chapter 22

"Used furniture?" Pender asked. "It was the one that was closed this week."

"How did you manage that?"

"The owner won an all-expense paid trip to New York to see the grand opening of *Titus* on Broadway."

"I'm guessing they are a big fan?"

"Wouldn't you know it? She's been acting on stage for years and dreamed of Broadway. The suddenness of the scheduled trip didn't give her enough time to schedule help to watch the store, so she closed it down for a week."

"Slick. You've gotten better at this."

I pointed to Kelen who was talking with Digger at the back of the store. "The kid has skills."

"And weird."

"What makes you say that?"

"The purple pants and the pink hair kind of speak for themselves."

I chuckled. "You may be right."

"You think?"

"I have a favor to ask," I said with a serious look. "If this goes south, I need you to get them out of there."

"We all know the score down there. They've got a whole pile of CIA goons and Frank fuckin' Steiner down there. If it goes south, we're probably all dead. All I can promise is I'll try. At least they don't have us all microchipped yet. You know they're chipping the BENT now."

"Dude, they're not putting microchips in the BENT."

"I'm tellin' you. Mark my words we'll all be chipped if they have their way. They started back in the late '90s."

Sometimes Pender was right but most times it was stuff like this. I just shook my head and walked toward the back of the store where Kelen was showing them the stairs into the basement.

"What?" Pender followed. "I'm serious. They started in the '90s. I knew a guy in Kentucky that dug one out of his…"

I tuned him out after he started giving examples. He was still talking as we followed the others into the basement.

The back wall was facing the Granite Mountain Materials which was the cover for the black sight.

Last time I was here I had to bury my brother. It wasn't disguised as a concrete company back then, it was just a warehouse structure in those days. They put a functioning business in its place several years later.

Jasper kept me from returning to clean the place out again when they came back to the site. I was still angry, but I had enough time to get to the point I could listen to him. It seemed like a waste of time as I grew older. They would always come back.

Digger pulled a can of spray paint from a bag he carried and painted an arch on the back wall of the basement.

"What the hell?" Pender asked. "Are you Wiley Coyote or something?"

"Helps to have an outline to go by." Digger shrugged.

Then he concentrated and clenched his fists. I could see the muscles bunch in his arms and neck as he strained for a moment. A small sound escaped him.

"Jesus, Digger, did you just strain out a fart?" Pender asked. "I thought you were gonna dig."

Digger chuckled. "Cyn, if you don't mind."

She stepped forward trying not to laugh and laid her hands on the cinder blocks. Her eyes glowed and the arch fell away as powder.

Behind the block was a straight tunnel in the shape of the arch that stretched close to fifty feet and angled down. It wasn't overly steep, but we had a long way to go so it didn't need to be.

"Damnit, man." Pender laughed. "You're not gonna do that every time are you?"

"Probably."

"Gonna get ripe in there."

Digger concentrated again and another section formed when the dirt slammed outward to solidify as the walls and ceiling of the tunnel.

Then he looked like he was about to do another one but stopped. "Nope, I'll be right back."

He walked out of the hole he had created and climbed the stairs.

"Where you goin'?" Pender asked.

"Bathroom."

Kel sat down in an antique chair. "This might take a while." He opened the laptop he brought in with him and pulled something else from his pocket, handing it to me. "Make yourself useful and point that down the tunnel."

I looked at the thing that looked like a scanner they use for cashiers and shrugged. Pointing it down the tunnel I pulled the trigger.

"Perfect." He turned the laptop around where I could see the screen which showed a 3D render of the tunnel as it was related to the black site. "He can ease off on the angle just a little, but he'll need to turn it a little to the left."

"How'd you do that?" Pender asked.

Kel pointed toward himself. "Not just a pretty face. What do you have going for you?"

"I can pick up a truck."

Kel nodded. "Okay, that counts."

I liked Pender even though he was crazy. Conspiracy theories get old after a while. Even if some of them were true, you never could tell what to believe because of the others.

"You doing alright, Cyn?" I asked as I sat down beside her against the side of the tunnel.

"Just tired, Alex." Her eyes still held some of the glow after absorbing the heavy particles from the wall. "I'm not as young as I used to be."

"Are you sure you're okay for this? I don't want you to hurt yourself."

"I hurt myself a long time ago, honey. I expect this isn't going to make things any worse."

I looked up as Digger walked back down the tunnel. Kelen stood and met him with the laptop, turning the screen toward him.

Digger looked at it for a minute and nodded. "Gotcha, kid."

"Kid? I'm forty years old."

"Heh."

"Never mind," Kelen said. "Fuckin geriatrics."

"I don't know what that means," Digger said. "But I'm too old to have some kid calling me names."

Kelen stared at him for a full minute before Digger chuckled and walked down the tunnel into the dark.

"Smart assed geriatrics," Kelen muttered.

"I'm going to the van for the lights," I said. "I'll be back shortly."

Two hours later we sat in the circle of light from the battery-powered shop light. Digger was sitting, leaning against the tunnel wall, head hanging down, softly snoring.

"He's taking a fuckin' nap?"

Kelen walked out of the darkness.

"We're old, kid." Pender shrugged and sat down across from me. "Part of the Gray Pride

Movement. We're here. We're old. Get off our lawn."

Kelen snorted.

"Speaking of gray pride, where've you been for the last twenty years, Lloyd? I mean the last few months have been obvious with all the news reports. The last thing I saw was some ruckus in Florida twenty-something years ago."

"The rumor mill said something about living with some revolutionaries in Mexico," Cynthia said. "Any truth to that?"

"It was Columbia," I said. "It was just a couple of years while everything cooled down after Florida."

"Why Columbia?" Pender asked.

"I had a close relationship with the leader of the resistance. Anna was really dedicated to—"

"Of course."

I looked at Cynthia. "What?"

"There was a girl. There's always a girl."

"I was there to help."

"Probably to help her out of her clothes," Digger said.

"About time you woke up. We've been sitting here forever," I said.

"Changing the subject?" she asked.

"Not at all. There's not always a girl."

"Sometimes it's a guy," Kelen said.

I took a breath to respond and Digger stood back up holding up a finger. "I'll be back."

Kelen sighed. "We needed Ocean's eleven and we got the Geriatric four."

Pender laughed. "If Ocean had these four, he'd never have needed eleven. You should have seen this bunch thirty-five years ago. Digger and Glow have pulled off some pretty impressive heists."

"What about you?" Kelen asked.

"I'm just good at beatin' people up."

"He was quite adept at distraction," Cynthia said. "He stacked a row of cars atop one another outside of that one place while we snatched a few jewels."

"A few?" Pender asked. "That was over a half million worth. We all lived pretty good that year."

"Those were the days. It was even easier when Alex joined us. He could go through the smallest places and leave no signs that anyone was there."

"Those were the days," I said, leaning back against the tunnel wall. "That jeweler was laundering money for some mob bosses, wasn't he?"

"It felt good to live off of the mob's money for a while," Cynthia said. "That was the one that began the setup for the lovely retirement I'm enjoying now."

"Red Hook is pretty nice," I said.

"Not as nice as that place Jasper got down in the Caribbean. I still don't know how he managed that without us knowing."

I glanced at Kelen who was hiding a smile.

"It's just a cabin on the beach," I said. "Nothing too fancy."

She stared at me for a minute. "You did that, didn't you? He never could save a thing. But I bet you did. You started as his protégé didn't you? It makes sense now."

I shrugged.

She smiled. "Thank you for that. He would have still been hustling people on the streets and he's too old for that. We hear from him occasionally. Usually, after the news goes on a tear about America's most wanted. He called last month to see if we'd heard anything."

"I talked with him after the Florida thing."

"You know most old people just do a book club or something," Kelen said. "You old farts get together and talk about this guy's antics. Well, I have one for you. Honey, you know that big art thing in Frisco that's been all over the news?"

"You're kidding me."
"I shit you not."
"Figures."

# Chapter 23

"This is it." Digger rested his hand on a concrete surface. "According to the kid, this is the lower right corner of the room holding the rock."

He drew a circle about eight inches across. "The rock is about six inches wide so it should fit in the bag."

"I'm heading out to the mouth of the tunnel so I can get set up as over-watch. Can't do shit from down here in this hole. I'll drop a couple of signal boosters on my way out so we can stay in contact." Kelen headed back up the tunnel.

We waited for about five minutes.

"Should be good to go," Kelen said on my earpiece.

"Alright, Cyn," I said. "Make a hole."

She laid her hand over the drawn circle and her eyes began to glow.

A fine dust settled to the bottom of the hole, and I looked inside where I could see light at the other end of about three feet of concrete.

"Let's take a look," I said as my head elongated and slipped into the hole followed by my body. I emulated a snake and slithered along the hole to stop close to the end.

"…clear…spoofed…" static crackled in my earpiece as Kelen checked in again.

The room looked clear, so I slid inside and looked at the rough chunk of rock. As I assumed a normal shape the static cleared.

"Do not go in! They spoofed the surveillance! Is anybody hearing me?"

"Fuck," I said as the glass wall in front of me cleared up.

There were several scientists, a large man standing in the middle of them, and four guys in suits with automatic rifles.

"Fuck me! Get out of there, Alex!" Kelen screamed. "Run!"

The wall to my left opened and a girl was shoved into the room. She was no more than a teen and her skin had golden scales.

How did we not know there was a test in progress?

The gunmen were as surprised as I was, and it took a few minutes to react. One of the scientists, hit an alarm while the other backpedaled toward the far wall. She wasn't interested in anything except getting away from the area in front of the glass.

They opened fire. I stepped between the girl and the hail of bullets and raised a thick shield to stop them. The mass it took left me lighter than it took to hold the shield steady, and the force of the gunfire took all of my strength to hold it up.

I staggered back and bumped into something. Fire filled my veins and strength I'd never felt thrummed through my body. The shield was light and still stopped the bullets. I stepped forward through the shattered glass just as the door burst open.

In the entrance stood a six-foot-tall blonde who looked like a football player.

"Fuck."

Steiner jumped forward and hit my shield, staggering me back through the glass. I needed more strength. And it was there, right out of the blue.

"Alex! Stop!" Cynthia's voice stopped me in my tracks.

Looking over my shield I gasped. Where Steiner had been was the lower half of a man. I glanced back to see a ragged hole in the wall and the table where the rock had been was gone. The golden-scaled girl was hugging the side wall just past the ragged hole. There was a crater in the floor that had a hole in the middle with light shining from below. The side wall where there had been three feet of concrete was gone and I was staring at three shocked faces.

I turned back toward the gunmen and with a thought, spikes sprang from my shield to pierce four hearts.

"You're the one behind all this." I pointed at the man in the middle.

"Listen, we can—" His voice halted as a spike shot through his left eye. I recognized the voice from the tapes.

I turned to the scientists. The woman who had backed away in the beginning held a phone which she dropped as my gaze settled on her.

My ears popped as someone appeared between me and her. I recognized him from the tapes we'd watched. The teleporter.

"I would appreciate it if you don't hurt Rebecca," he said with his hands outstretched in front of him. "She was helping me."

I stopped moving toward them. "Helping you what?"

"Destroy the rock."

I glanced behind me. "Where is it?"

Cynthia swallowed and pointed at me.

"What?"

"You did this."

"What?"

"When the wall went down, it was flowing into you."

I looked toward the terrified girl against the wall. She nodded quickly. "It went into you."

"Fuck."

There was an electrical zap from the computer console and Kelen materialized beside the other scientist. His fists were glowing with electricity as he looked for someone to hit.

"I thought you said clear," I said.

"I said the room is not clear, dumbass! Their cyber guy spoofed all the surveillance. Motherfucker won't be doing that again. What happened?" He saw the bottom half of Steiner still standing upright in front of me with the area just above the waist cauterized. "What the—"

"I'd suggest we get out of here first," the teleporter said. "I can take us all somewhere we can figure out what's happening."

His face was familiar to me even though we'd never met, and I hadn't seen his face in the recordings. I couldn't quite place it, though.

"Alright, but if you try to screw us, you'll not survive it either."

"I'm not one of the bad guys," he said and pointed at the dead men. "They were. And there are three hundred more of them in this base."

I turned to look back at Cynthia, Digger, and Pender. Cynthia gave me a small nod. I turned back to the teleporter. "Then let's go."

My ears popped again, and sand blew in my face. I was staring out across the desert. I glanced behind me to see all of them still there, including the girl. Kelen was in front of me naked as the day he was born, and the lightning died out in his fists.

"Shit. There's no connection out here."

"Sorry about that," the teleporter said. "I've never moved that many people at once. Had to go somewhere familiar."

He pointed at me. "And you weigh a damn ton."

I shifted my shield back inside and resumed the form I had been using. It was instant, unlike any time before I had been knocked back into the rock. A fine red dust filled the air around me.

"That's new," I said and turned around to find Cynthia holding the sides of her head.

"Cyn?"

"The…glow…"

"Jesus! What is it?"

"I can… release it. All… of it… Get away!" Her eyes began to glow brighter than I'd ever seen them.

"We need to get away from her!" I said to the teleporter and my ears popped again.

We were further out in the desert. I spun around until I could see her tiny form in the distance. Then the horizon lit up like the sun.

"Cyn!"

Pender took a step in her direction and leapt thirty feet to tumble and roll.

"The hell?"

"It's you," Digger said. "When you shifted there was that dust. I bet it's part of the rock. I feel better than I have in years. Cyn just released the glow. She's never been able to do that. Pender just stepped thirty feet. And the kid over there is looking a bit squirrelly."

I looked toward Kelen who had a dazed expression on his face. "Kel!"

He turned to me and smiled. "I can feel them."

"What?"

"Satellites."

"It's Cyn!" Pender yelled, pointing toward the fading light. She was still there.

I was afraid to move after that last shift. The girl with the scales had dropped to a seated position with a look of amazement on her face. I wasn't sure what she was going through but it seemed to be something she liked.

A hand landed on my back. "Damage is already done," the teleporter said. "It doesn't hit twice. I've touched the rock several times after the change. I couldn't lift it though. It weighed a lot. Wasn't sure I could teleport something that heavy. I'm still new to this."

I took a step toward Cynthia and hurtled through the air like Pender had done.

"You still have most of that mass." The teleporter said as he appeared beside me. "I wouldn't try shifting for a little bit. By the way, the name's Adam. Adam LeMonte."

"I guess you figured out who I am already?"

"Yeah, I believe so," he said. "You're the guy mom told me about."

"Mom?"

"Deadre LeMonte."

"You're Deadre's kid?"

"Yeah. She said my dad was a guy she met in college that she used to party with. Said he was wanted by the authorities and had to leave when the cops got onto who he was. You're him, aren't you? Alex Lloyd?"

I stood there with my mouth hanging open.

Kelen erupted with laughter.

"I'll go get your friend… Dad. And *you* need some clothes." He nodded toward Kelen and disappeared.

"Fuck."

# Chapter 24

"How did they fool you?" I asked as I slowly raised the coffee cup to my lips.

"Their cyber guy. He detected one of my trips into the system and spoofed everything after that. I found it when I got out of the tunnel and physically went into the system. I tried to warn you."

"Yeah."

"I, for one, am pleased with the results," Cynthia said. "I feel like a new woman."

"Was that all the glow you'd stored up over the years?" I asked.

"It was. I was never able to release it before."

"You look a great deal better," I said. "It took twenty years or more off your appearance."

"It feels like it too. I'm going to the doctor next week to see if it might have given me those twenty years back or it just feels like it did."

"It's going to take me some time to get used to the added strength from the boost," Pender said, holding the broken handle from the coffee cup in his hand. "How are you not breaking things?"

"I have to adapt to added strength every time I shift smaller. I'm used to it. It's never been anything like this before though. I'm afraid to drop the mass since a lot of it is the rock. There's no telling what the effects would be. The rock killed normal people although, when I shifted, it didn't affect the scientist, Rebecca. Right now, I'm afraid to shift at all."

"You have to do it sometime," Cynthia said. "We've already been affected. It will be better if you have someone near."

"At least the kid's wearing clothes now, if you can call it that."

"Honey, *these* are Louis Vuitton."

"Never heard of him. I've read some Louis L'Amour but never heard of this Vuitton fella."

Kelen sighed and shook his head. "Savages."

"Did anyone get the dragon kid's name?" I asked. "She just hugged me as soon as we were back in the states and turned into a dragon. Flew away."

"At least she wasn't mad at you. She might have tried to breathe fire on you." Pender said.

"True enough."

"Where did Adam, Digger, and Rebecca go?" Pender asked.

"Digger wanted to go home and get some rest," Cynthia said. "His Talent was boosted like the rest of us, but it did nothing for his fatigue after the tunnel. Adam teleported him back home. The scientist was afraid to be left here with America's most wanted so she went with them."

"Do you believe her story?" I asked.

"After seeing the videos of what that man threatened others with, I think I do," she said. "I wouldn't doubt that she was coerced."

"I feel about the same."

Kelen put his cup down. "I need to get back to LA. I have to do some public relations after this latest caper. They're going to try to hit the air with another terrorist attack by America's most wanted and I'm about to go release a bunch of videos of them killing people. I may even release the copy of what happened in that room when we got there."

"I think the others will be enough. Especially after they blow up the terrorist thing."

"Alright." He raised his cup and put it back down. "You got this?"

"Yup."

In a flash of electricity, he was gone, Louis Vuitton suit and all.

"He's happy to be able to travel dressed now," Cynthia said.

"Yup. He spent most of this whole thing running around naked."

"At least Pender gave him a shirt."

"I got tired of seein' him run around with his junk floppin' around," Pender said.

"Just jealous." Cynthia grinned.

He grunted. "What I wouldn't give to be that age again."

"Wouldn't we all?" I asked.

"What are you going to do now, Alex?" Cynthia asked.

"I don't know yet. I have to get used to this all over again and I can't do it surrounded by people as long as the damn rock keeps changing people. Thinking about going north. Maybe Alaska this time."

"This time?"

"Spent a few years in Canada. Nice people. Except in Vancouver. They're assholes in Vancouver."

She just shook her head with an eyebrow raised. "What?"

"Nothing. Just marveling at your weirdness. I, for one, am done with the life of Talents and Bends. I'm going home to Red Hook and enjoy my retirement."

"Me too," Pender said. "The kid says he purged any record that had our faces from the databases at the black site. I didn't really do anything except see some of my theories come true. I got a hell of a boost in strength though, so thanks, buddy."

I nodded. "Just be careful with it."

"I will. I did this once a long time ago. I can manage to do it again."

"I seem to remember a lot of damage left behind you back then."

"Shhh… Don't say that kind of thing. You'll hurt my feelings."

"Yeah, and then comes the inordinate amount of damage."

"Heh! At least I don't get hurt feelings like I did back then. Once you hit your sixties, you don't have time for all that."

"I guess it's time for me to disappear again, kids. You alright to get back home?"

"Sure thing. Adam is going to meet us later today and drop us off. You're not going to stay and see him?"

"I'm still trying to wrap my head around that part. I may stop in Chicago and see Deadre on my way north. By then I should have it worked out."

Cynthia laughed. "Good luck there, my friend."

"I'll probably need all the luck I can get." I stood up from the metal booth that creaked under me. "I have to get somewhere and get rid of some of this weight. I can't even sit in a regular chair."

Pender laughed. "Welcome to the super strength club."

"Thanks again for helping. You know how to get in touch with Kel. He can reach me. If you need anything…"

I slowly walked out of the diner, careful not to break anything. It would suck to be like this all the time. I always enjoyed the higher strength from condensing my form, but this was ridiculous. I was close to a half-ton of condensed mass which put me above Pender in strength at the moment. It was obvious from my last shift that I could expel mass as well as absorb it now. I could theoretically turn into a car with the body mass I had. A compact car. But a car.

I was going to have to find out what the limits were to my Talent. And that was going to take isolation. And I needed to figure out what absorbing that chunk of the asteroid was going to do to me. It wasn't still boosting my Talent if Adam had been correct. It was a one-shot thing. But I had absorbed it into my being. Could I expel it as a whole or was I fated to put off this talent-boosting dust whenever I shifted?

Annoyed with Lloyd

# Chapter 25

dam had brought us to Georgia when we came back from the desert in Afghanistan. I think he'd spent some time there in the Army.

"My kid in the Army?" I chuckled.

I wasn't sure how that had happened. I guess his DNA only had some of the markers or they didn't test their DNA. I stayed away from the government when I could manage so I didn't know as much about how they did things. I had no doubt that the Army and the CIA were quite different. All the letter agencies were divisions of the CIA, but the armed forces were their own and not under goon squad control.

I had seen several of the agencies in action over the years, the FBI was in control of domestic issues with no ties to the BENT. The NSA was in charge of the security of the nation. But the CIA was the umbrella that covered them all. They could step in at any time and take over like they did in Florida when I swam up the damn coast to Georgia.

I'm sure there were some good people who worked for them, but my experiences were with people who would lobotomize close to fifty people because they were telepaths or murder that many people to see what this stupid rock would do.

So far, I had zero uses for them.

The scientist had stayed as far away from me as she could, so I didn't know much about her except she was helping Adam. I had Kelen let me watch the videos again and saw her in several of them. She was present and working with them as they killed a bunch of people. I wasn't sure if she deserved any better treatment than they did. When your job is to do what they were doing, you quit the job. I didn't know her story, so I left that judgment up to my son.

My son. Holy shit. I had a son. I think.

I remembered the times Deadre and I had been together, and I could see the possibilities. Usually, I was my own contraceptive but there were times when lightning had been striking all around when I could have lost my concentration. Maybe when the tornado dropped around us that time.

"Weather witches," I muttered. I stopped and sat on a bus bench. "What are you gonna do?"

"Excuse me?"

I was sitting close enough to a woman who heard me. She was red -haired, freckled, and quite pretty.

"Sorry," I said. "Just musing about past decisions."

"Oh, I thought you called me a weather witch."

"Really?"

"My students have taken to calling me that. I'm trying to place you, but I don't remember you in any of my classes."

I chuckled. "You at the University?"

"I am. I teach meteorology."

"I went to college a long time ago. Even took some meteorology classes in Chicago."

"Chicago… Oh, then you were talking about *the* Weather Witch."

"I was. I guess if you teach it you've heard of her."

"Absolutely. I always wanted to *be* her as I grew up. Did you know she cleared up the storms in Illinois last month just to let the Emperor land?"

"I saw on the news she offered to."

"They gave her the go-ahead. Chicago didn't want to miss out on his visit. It's a little exciting seeing him out in public. I don't expect him to come down here."

"I don't either," I said wondering how old she was to be excited for a mass murderer to be doing a tour. "So, they call you that cause you teach it or is there another reason?"

She was a little hesitant.

"Don't worry about me, I'm as BENT as they come." I touched the bus stop signpost and pinched the metal slightly together with my thumb and forefinger.

I didn't want to break the thing and get arrested.

"Oh…"

"Yeah."

"You're not just BENT but a Talent?"

"Talents are assholes, I'm just BENT."

She laughed. "I can do stuff in a small scale like a greenhouse or something. Nothing like LeMonte. She can work weather across states or even countries."

"She has a lot of power. They keep her from doing much though."

"A lot of damage can be done in a short time when altering weather. She had to work another day to fix the patterns after letting the plane land. I've heard of some of her mishaps from the old days when she just started learning how to use her powers."

"I was there and saw a few of them firsthand."

"No way! You can't be that old. You look like a twenty-something."

"I'm a little older than I look," I said. "I knew Deadre when she was taking those same weather classes I took. I actually took them because she wanted me to."

"Oh, you were close?"

"Dated a little while. She was determined to become a superhero and I didn't want any of that life, so we went our separate ways."

"That is truly amazing," she said. "What are the odds you'd sit down on the same bench as me?"

"It's a funny world. I've met a few really nice people by just sitting and talking to strangers. I travel a lot, so I meet strangers pretty often."

"Well, I'm Andy, Andy Riale. Now we're not strangers."

"Benjamin Tyler," I said. "And it's nice to meet you, Andy."

She was biting her lower lip as she thought for a moment. "You know I don't usually do this, but would you like to get a drink?"

I had no doubt that was a very bad idea. "I'd love to."

Annoyed with Lloyd

# Chapter 26

"…Athens, Georgia where the abnormal weather over the last few days has settled and we are here with the one responsible. It seems a young meteorology teacher with a minor Talent has become a major Talent overnight…

I sat up in the bed. I was in a motel just over the state line into Kentucky.

"… Hasn't been a weather witch of this caliber since Deadre LeMonte hit the scene in the '90s. Miss Riale, can you explain what happened?"

The camera swung to the reporter's left.

"Fuck." I said.

"I don't even know if I can explain it except… thank you, Benjamin Tyler!"

There was a lightning strike a little ways from the crew and a loud roll of thunder.

"Sorry," Andy said in a meek voice as she bounced excitedly.

There was an electrical sound and Kelen materialized in the only chair the room had.

"Are you shittin' me?" he motioned toward the TV. "On your own for less than a day and you did this?"

I sighed. "I knew it was a bad idea but look at her."

He shook his head. "Can't keep it in your pants, can you?"

"I never shifted the whole time. How did it get to her?"

"You ever thought of using a condom?"

"Oh."

"Yeah, oh. You just found out you have a kid, and you decide to go off and try to get another one the next day."

"I've always been my own contraceptive," I said. "I don't send live swimmers."

"But it's still a part of you. And I'm guessing that rock has permeated all of you since you absorbed it. And I beg to differ. Meeting your son means you don't always get the contraceptive right."

"She dropped a damned tornado down on top of us. Forgive me if I lost my concentration a little."

He looked up and seemed to be searching for a moment. "Jesus, Alex. Thirty-one years ago, a random F4 dropped just north of Chicago and stayed in one spot for over an hour. That's what you're talking about?"

I grinned. "You digging the new power level?"

"It is nice to be able to take my clothes with me for a change. I don't have to depend on you to buy me the right things."

"You're wearing the Louis Vuitton I got you."

"Even a broken clock is right twice a day."

"Heh. I like that one."

"The suit?" he asked.

"No, the saying. That suit's horrid. You need to get a nice Armani without a hole in the back where someone got stabbed. Then you'd have to drive the ladies off with a stick."

"What if I'm not after ladies?"

"I won't judge. You've met me, right? But it goes for them too. Everybody's crazy about a sharp dressed man."

"If you're gonna quote lyrics to me you should get them right."

"If they wrote it today, that's what it would say."

"Probably." He shrugged. "I guess I need to scrub the Tyler ID and redo your background. I wish you could stay out of trouble for a minute so I can leave one of these intact for longer than a week. You used to go months or even years without needing to change. Ever since the warehouse was hit, I'm putting together shit right and left."

"I had ten or so identities tied up in the stuff inside the warehouse. I used them anytime I needed to change on the go. Now I need some new ones. Least you get paid for them."

"Speaking of getting paid, when are you doing a new job?"

"I just gave you a bag full of money."

"Sweetie, that was last month. What have you done for me lately?"

"I had a big old diamond, but I absorbed it. I can't do anything where I have to change for a while. When I get up north where I'm away from everyone I'll see if I can get this damn rock out of me. I already found out I can expel mass. Maybe if I shift enough, I can get rid of it. Problem is I can't do it anywhere with people around or we get something like Athens."

"Shifting has nothing to do with what happened in Athens. You couldn't keep it in your pants, and it looks like there are several other ways to expel mass."

"Well, there's one other way, anyway."

"Where was this diamond?" he changed the subject back to money.

"It was in my pocket."

"You were walking around with a diamond in your pocket?"

"Well, yeah. Where else was I gonna carry it?'

He shook his head. "How big a diamond?"

I held my hand up with the fingers about an inch and a half apart.

He rubbed his forehead. "You're killing me, man."

"I picked it up at the storage building in Frisco. Donny got curious and went looking for the first thing I ever stole, figuring it would be a baseball card or a comic book."

"The first thing you ever stole was a diamond the size of a walnut?"

"Well, yeah. The asteroid was coming, and we were all gonna die anyway. No one was even at the shop when I did it. Everyone was home with their loved ones."

"Sometimes I forget how old you are. There aren't many still alive that weren't just babies who were there to see it."

"Close to seventy years ago," I said. "I was twenty-five when it hit."

"You still act like you're twenty-five."

"I even feel like I am now, too. Whatever the stone did to me, it was good. I don't feel like I'm barely holding together anymore. I was having to concentrate harder and harder to get the shapes right. Now I have to concentrate to not shift with a thought. I should have just gotten Adam to port me to Alaska, but we've been avoiding one another since he told me I was his dad. I'm going to see Deadre to be sure before heading north. But I know he's mine. He has my brother's eyes."

He nodded and was quiet for a few moments.

"Can I ask you one thing?"

"Sure."

"Why were you still carrying a diamond the size of a walnut in your pocket while we were breaking into one of the most secure places in the country?"

"I didn't want to just leave it laying around."

He sighed.

"What?"

"Nothing. Nothing at all."

# Chapter 27

After Kelen left I sat around for several hours watching the news. It didn't take long for me to realize why I hated it so much. They always focus on the sensational. Everything was about ratings. It seemed like an endless cycle of murder, BENTs, and politicians. There was always a story about the BENT. Several stations covered the thing in Athens. Andy Riale had become an overnight sensation.

In hindsight, I should have left the hotel immediately. She burned the Tyler identity on national TV.

Instead, I was half asleep when the door of my room exploded inward. I snapped awake to see a familiar face. I wasn't sure where I'd seen the guy before though.

"Uh… just come on in, I guess."

The black man was over six feet tall and large.

"I will," he said. "Here's the part where you can save yourself a lot of pain. Give me the rock."

"Oh! That's where I saw you before. You were one of the bouncers at that club in Portland. I knew I'd seen you before."

"Just give me the rock and I can let you live."

"Well, there's a problem with that."

He took a step forward and I stood up. "See, I don't actually have the rock."

Another person stepped into the room behind the bouncer.

"I see where this is going. Necromancer guy, um… Jerry? Nah wasn't that. Jared! Like the sub sandwich guy."

"You're awful glib for a man who's about to die, Mister Lloyd."

"That escalated really fast," I said. "You don't even give a guy time to think about it?"

"I don't need you breathing to tell me everything I need to know."

"Remember he said that, bouncer guy. When you go back to Milo, you tell him that this is *not* my fault."

"Davis, just kill him so I can interrogate the corpse."

"Jerry, you're really making this next part easy."

Davis strode forward and swung at me. I wasn't in the largest form I'd used before but the mass I had condensed into it was outrageous. I caught the enormous fist with a single hand that was half the size of the bouncer's. The impact shattered the room's window and the concrete floor below me even vibrated.

"That's a solid swing you got there, Davis."

Jared Khan's mouth dropped open as he didn't see the expected result.

I slowly looked around the big man in front of me where Jared was drawing a big revolver from a holster on his side.

"Alright," I said and grabbed the big man's arm.

I pulled forward and swung him in a circle, releasing him to crash through the front wall. There was blood on both the ceiling and the floor where the Necromancer had been standing.

I stepped forward and poked my head through the shattered concrete wall. "Jerry? Are you okay?"

I stepped through the wall and paused as I remembered I was still undressed. My skin fluctuated and reformed as a black suit.

"Holy shit…"

There was a groan from across the parking lot where the bouncer was trying to pull himself from the truck he was embedded in.

As he staggered forward, I grimaced. The concrete wall was also embedded in the truck as well as a gruesome-looking mess.

"Jerry?"

The bouncer turned and collapsed to his knees in front of the truck.

I walked across the lot and stopped in front of Davis who was looking at his former boss.

"I don't think he's okay," I said as I raised him back to his feet. "Now you need to tell Milo that this wasn't my doing. Jerry was an asshole and refused to even talk to me. He brought this on you both."

"Khan will kill me if I go back with this."

"You tell him I can't give him the rock. It's gone. Destroyed."

"He'll never believe that. And you just killed his brother. He'll hunt you down wherever you go."

"So be it. He can join the crowd. Now go. And when he comes hunting, make sure you're not with him. I see you again it'll get a lot bloodier." I pointed toward the road.

He staggered three cars down and got into an SUV. As he drove out of the parking lot, I walked straight to the Suburban I had been driving and got into the driver's seat. Kelen had changed all the tracks to the truck earlier, so it was relatively safe.

I drove out of the lot and turned west. Khan would be after me soon enough I needed to shift and didn't want to in the city. First, I would need to ditch the truck, just in case. Kelen did clean work, but I remembered that guy they called the Technomancer. I figured he was the one that sent these guys as quickly as they came. I walked away from the Suburban at a truck stop outside of Louisville and hitched a ride with a truck driver.

"Where you headed, honey?" The metal-skinned trucker asked. She gleamed in the reflection of headlights across the lot.

"Chicago, if you're heading that way."

"Gotta stop in Rockford. I can get you that far."

"That would be great."

"Climb in."

I walked around and climbed into the passenger side. The air seat sank almost all the way as I sat down.

She smiled. "I was pretty sure you were one of those."

"Those?"

"Strength Bend."

"I guess you could say that. What gave me away?"

"The way you sat on that concrete bench like you might break it."

"Heh."

"But I'm right."

"True enough."

"What do you weigh?"

"That seems a bit personal."

She laughed. "Just need to make sure it doesn't affect the load limit at the scales."

"Actually, I don't know."

"Maybe we should swing through the truck scales behind the depot there and find out."

"Alright. What's all that metal weigh?"

"You never ask a lady her weight."

"You have a point."

"Nine hundred and eighty-six."

"Wow."

"What?"

"Just thinking that's a lot of woman in an impressive package." I was grinning. "You weighing me up for something else perhaps?"

"Pretty sure of yourself."

"Just curious."

She smiled as we pulled onto the scales.

# Chapter 28

"Just how strong are you?" Ginger asked, shifting down gears for the grade ahead. It was a little steep and her truck was loaded heavy.

"I don't really know," I said.

"I doubt that. Everyone who's got a strength Bend tests their limits at some point. You have to if you want to be able to walk around like a regular person."

"It's not really that simple," I said. "But I don't mind testing it if you want."

"You really don't know? Oh Lord, did you just get your Bend?"

"That doesn't happen all that often anymore. Most Bends are triggered at puberty. There are some that happen later in life, and I've even heard of a few kids born with it. I've been BENT for a long time. The strength is new though."

"If you don't want to explain it, that's fine but how do you get super strength after already being BENT? I could use that. I'm looking at a rough future as it is."

"Rough?"

"You've heard of MMA fighting? How they banned any Bends in the ring?"

"Yeah, BENT fights went underground. Are you tangled up in that? I like to gamble some, but I never wagered on the underground fights. It's too chancy."

"Well, I'm not a gambler."

"You're a fighter?"

"I am. I never wanted to be in the business, just kind of fell into it. I'd like to get out, but it doesn't work that way. They bring you in and sink their claws, then they don't let you walk away. They have enforcers that keep a tight leash on you and then there are the *other* ways. They always get something to hold over your head."

"Sounds tough."

"It is what it is. I try to leave, and they show fight footage to the cops, and we all know what happens then. I'm very recognizable and I end up arrested for illegal fighting and a trip straight to the Crypt."

"Nobody wants to go to the Crypt," I said. "That place is a great big black hole for the BENT."

"I don't know much about it except they manage to hold some guys I didn't think could be held. They have Wreckage inside that hole."

I chuckled.

"What?"

"Wreckage. Frank Steiner."

"You act like you know Steiner."

"Don't worry about Steiner. I don't think he's going to be an issue anymore."

"You know something?"

"I know Steiner's gone. We can leave it at that."

"How would you even know that? There's no news out of the Crypt."

"I have sources that I trust that say he went after someone he shouldn't and ended up dead."

"Sources? That can get information out of the Crypt?"

"My source can get information from pretty much anywhere," I said. "You got a cell phone I can use?"

We reached the bottom of the grade, and she started shifting up, the truck lurched with each shift that did wonderful things to parts of her anatomy.

She laughed as she saw what I was watching. "Cell is on the dash."

"Sorry, I got distracted."

"I see that."

"The whole living metal thing amazes me. Everything moves just like it normally would."

She smiled and shifted gears.

I moved a couple of things on the dash until I found the cell phone and dialed a number.

"Sweetie, you *have* to quit calling me every five minutes."

"How'd you know it was me?"

"You *still* don't understand what it is that I do."

"Probably never will. I might have a line on a job here."

"Do tell."

I looked at Ginger. "Where's this thing at?"

"Rockford."

I nodded. "I need everything you can get on an underground fighting ring in Rockford, Illinois. BENT fighting."

"You know I hate that shit."

"Thought we might burn it down."

"Well, *now* you're talking. I'll call back in a few. Tell your trucker lady not to be surprised when I show up suddenly."

"Now I'm a little worried. You stalking me?"

"No, but I did a check as soon as I saw the number. Of course, it goes to a pretty lady made of metal who drives a truck."

"Hmm."

"Keep it in your pants."

"Bye now," I said and hung up.

I placed the cell back on the dash and turned to Ginger who had a worried look on her face.

"Burn it down? They have a lot of incriminating evidence on a lot of people."

"When we burn something down, we burn it."

"I'm beginning to wonder just who the hell you really are."

"Isaac Sanders, at least for the moment."

Annoyed with Lloyd

# Chapter 29

"This one is the place I stay when I'm in town. They have some extras for BENT customers like me. Sturdy beds and cast iron tubs."

She was turning down a small road beside a medium-sized one story motel outside of Rockford. There was a decent-sized lot in the back where she found ample room to park the rig.

"I've stayed in a lot worse," I said. "It's not overly fancy though."

"It's a trucker motel," she said. "Don't be surprised if you get propositioned on the way to the room."

"Okay."

"That didn't seem to bother you at all."

"I told you I've stayed in worse. One story is good with the weight, I have to watch out where I go."

"It's hard to believe you weigh twelve hundred pounds."

"I know. Right?"

"How long ago was it you got this Bend? I swear you act like it was yesterday."

I thought for a moment. "Uh, six days."

"Six days?"

"Well, closer to seven at the moment."

"How are you even functioning?"

"Very carefully."

She shook her head. "I was thirteen when my Bend hit. It took me weeks to get any control of it. You're this settled after six days?"

"I've been adapting to different levels longer than I even want to think about. This is just another level."

"I still don't understand you."

"I'm a shapeshifter. When I go small, I still have the same mass and have to adapt to another strength level. When I turn a three-hundred-pound man into the size of a ninety-pound woman, she's pretty strong. So, I adapt. I was eight inches tall about a month ago and kicked a hole in a block wall. I'm used to adapting."

"How did you end up like this?"

"This?" I motioned toward myself. "This is new. I was always constrained to a certain mass. And, um, now I'm not."

"Shift something," she said.

"I can't."

She let out a slow breath.

"I know. It's frustrating as hell. I can shift with a thought, but I have to concentrate pretty hard to keep from doing it."

"Why don't you?"

"This whole mass thing is new. Now I can absorb mass and I can expel mass but it's dangerous to do it."

"Dangerous?"

"I absorbed something dangerous. I can't expel it until I get far enough away from people that it won't do any damage."

"Then why are you here with me?"

"You need help. That's kind of what I do."

"What kind of dangerous is it?"

"It was a solid piece of the asteroid that fell in '54. It changes Bends. Amplifies things. With Talents, it does some powerful changes. The BENT might become Talents. We don't really know what the effects are on others. The rock killed normal people but not the BENT. My shifting releases some of it but I don't know the repercussions of that yet. It didn't kill a normal who was there the one time I did it, but it amplified four Talents and made a BENT girl with scales able to turn into a dragon."

She was staring at me with a worried expression.

"Yeah, it's some weird shit. I know. We gonna get a room?"

She nodded and opened her door. "I'll get the room, but I don't know about that story."

I shrugged. "It is what it is."

It was somewhere between five and ten minutes until she walked back around the corner and returned to the truck. Reaching into the back, she dragged a bag out of the sleeper.

"I guess I'll risk it," she said. "Got us a room back here. Room thirty-one on the corner over there."

"I almost expected you to call the cops."

"What good would that do me? I think you may be my way out of this whole thing. I can't see passing up the opportunity."

"Then we'll see about making a plan," I said and climbed down from the truck.

# Chapter 30

"What happens when you boost a talent?" Ginger asked from the bathroom.

I was sitting in the chair in the corner of the room. "So far it depends. Talents become stronger, Bends seem to progress in whatever direction they were going before they stopped. I've seen the videos of the people touching the rock but the way I seem to do it is maybe diluted some. It killed regular folks who touched it, but the lady scientist wasn't affected when I shifted. We really don't know much about how it works."

"What would it do to my Bend?"

"I don't know. It might make you stronger, it might turn the metal into real steel instead of living steel. I have no clue."

"Might make me stronger, might kill me?"

"Pretty much. We don't really know what your Bend would do as a progression. The kid with scales turned into a dragon. She could have just as easily turned into a gecko. I'll admit, the dragon was much cooler. There was a lady I met in LA with a beard. What would her Bend progress into? Would she be fully covered if it progressed? I don't know what the thing is going to do. It's been inside me for six days. It's dangerous to test it on other people."

"What if I volunteered?"

"Why?"

"This match they have set up next week isn't just a match."

"What do you mean?"

"They're making me fight their champion. He's a strength Bend guy that's never been beaten. Thing is, they're all working for Darv. He's mean and they do what he tells them. I worry about what he'll tell the champ to do."

"What do you think they'll tell him to do?"

"They know I want out. What if they tell him to kill me? I'm in for a hell of a beating, regardless. Strength Bends heal slow."

"Is he that much stronger?"

"I think so. If I lose a fight, it's one thing but what if they want to get rid of me?"

"All I can say is we can try if you want to but it's a crap shoot what the outcome will be. It may kill you, too."

"It's worth a shot."

"Is it?"

"Yes. Listen, I don't have anyone that would miss me if it did kill me. Who wants a woman like this?"

"Jesus Christ, woman. You're a marvel. Why wouldn't anyone want you?"

"I'm made of metal. I burn hot when I move. Have you ever touched a hot frying pan? When metal moves it generates heat."

"That causes problems of its own I imagine."

"See," she said. "But if it made me strong enough to win this match, I could make a ton of money as the underdog. Maybe enough to get away from this place and this life."

"What if someone just gave you the money you need to leave?"

"That's not exactly the same as taking it from the people that have been blackmailing me for five years. Besides, I don't have those kind of friends."

"I'll do it if you really want this, but I can also give you the money to leave if you want."

"You? The guy hitching a ride at a truck stop?"

I shrugged.

"I'll take the boost. How do you do it?"

"First, we can't do it in here. I don't know how long the area would be affected. I would need to shift because the other way, although much more fun, is probably out of the question. Strong or not, I can still feel the heat so it would probably be too hot."

"What do you mean?"

"As Kel said the other day, there's more than one way to expel mass."

She started to say something and stopped with her mouth open. "Oh…"

"Yeah. If you heard the news recently, there's a new Weather Witch in Athens Georgia."

"That was you? And you and her…"

"Um, yeah." I shrugged again. "Now don't get me wrong. If you want to, I'll give it a shot. Not sure about the whole frying pan thing, and you're gorgeous so we can rip our clothes off and roast some nuts…"

She snorted and sat down in the reinforced chair beside the desk. "I'd prefer not to roast you even if I *do* want to try it. It's been a long time."

"If I could shift right now, I'd turn metal and we could do some welding."

"You say the sweetest things."

"Heh. If you want to do this, we need to go out away from any population and do it. Like I said, I don't know how long the particular area is affected."

"I want to try it."

"Kel's going to kill me. But let's get this party started."

"So how does this work?" she said as we sat on a rock ledge looking out over the valley below. "Do I need to do anything?"

"First take off all the clothes," I said.

She unbuttoned the top button of her shirt and I grinned. "Just kidding. You just sit there and try to remain still after I shift. If your power boosts, you may need to ease into it."

She snorted and buttoned it back. "Missed your chance."

I laughed. "Might be good to move back from this ledge too. I'm perfectly fine with doing this naked if you want to though."

We stood and moved back from the ledge.

"Alright let's do this," she said.

I shifted into someone pretty close to Isaac's form and tried not to lose much mass along the way. A fine red dust filled the air around me and drifted down. I looked toward Ginger to see her eyes widen as the change occurred.

She staggered as things altered that I couldn't see. Then she looked up at me. "Is it done?"

I nodded. "Try to take a step away from the ledge."

She stepped forward a single step. "It feels the same. But something is different. I can feel it. Something I need to reach for…"

The change started in her hands as they were held out in front of her. The steel seemed to fade away leaving a pale white skin underneath.

"Holy shit," I said. "You're changing back to flesh."

The change sped up as she realized what was happening and really reached for that thing she felt.

When she finished, she stood there with her mouth hanging open.

"Are you okay?" I asked.

"I'm not metal. It's gone!" she looked thoughtful. "But it's not either. It's right there where I can feel it. I can change!"

She smiled in amazement and the next thing I knew she was in my arms. "Thank you! Thank you! Thank you!" Her flesh and blood lips connected with mine. "Thank you, Isaac Sanders, or whatever your name is. This changes everything."

"It does." I let her step back. "You can have that life you missed, now."

"But the fight…"

I shifted again. I was standing in front of her as a metal reflection. "You don't need to worry about that anymore. This time next week it won't be a problem."

"But how did you…?"

"I'll be in that ring next week and they're in for a rude awakening. Let's get back to the motel and I'll get Kel to fix you up. You just go live that life you should have been able to. I'm going to have to get some details so I can be as convincing as you when I get to them."

"That is so weird hearing that in my voice. Oh, does another shift affect me?"

"Nope, it's one and done."

"Oh, thank God. I thought for just a second I would change again."

"You should be okay."

"That means the other way wouldn't affect me either?"

"It wouldn't."

"It's a shame you already turned into me."

The metal faded and I was flesh again. A little dust drifted in the air.

She giggled. "You're still a woman." Then she looked down and her eyes widened. "Oh my God. Wow."

"I can be whatever you want. We just have to do the shifts here. I already messed this spot up and I don't know how long its effect stays."

A slow smile crept across her face. "This is good," she said and stepped back into my arms. "It's crazy but I…think I like it. Who *are* you?"

"Nobody important."

"Sure," she said before our lips met again.

# Chapter 31

"What did I tell you?"

I opened my eyes to find Kelen sitting in the chair of our room. He wore a leopard print single piece something. His short cropped hair was dyed red.

"It's worse every time," I said.

His eyes turned from Ginger, who he thought was me. They narrowed slightly. "What gets worse?"

"Nothing."

Kellen pointed at the blonde-haired trucker still snoring lightly beside me. "What happened? Where's the metal lady? And what happened to keeping it in your pants?"

I flipped back the cover where I was female and naked except for the metal. "I don't have one to keep in my pants."

"Smart ass, If you're her, where's the trucker?"

I motioned toward the sleeping blonde.

Kelen raised an eyebrow as Ginger opened her eyes and looked slightly confused.

"You must be his friend."

"Friend might be pushing it just a little, sweetie."

She chuckled and sat up, the covers falling down. She spun her legs to the side and stood up.

"Definitely not shy," he said.

"I'm a truck driver."

She walked right by him and entered the bathroom where I heard the water start running into the large cast iron tub.

"How is she not metal?" he asked. "I was pretty sure she was always metal."

"The boost was different this time," I said. "She can change back and forth now. The plan was for her to boost her strength and we'd bet a ton of money on her as the underdog in this next fight, but her strength wasn't boosted."

"So, what now? I assume since you look like her, you plan to take her place?"

"Yeah."

"You know it's a bad idea, right? You can't shift in there. There's a whole building full of BENT in that place."

"I figured."

"You have to concentrate not to shift and now fight an MMA fighter with super strength at the same time. I checked the fighting ring out. They're really pushing this match on the dark web. They plan to kill this girl and do it on film. The regular crowd of viewers aren't even a part of this one. There's a group of VIPs that are paying a lot to see this 'snuff film' when Jack Savage kills her."

"Jack Savage?"

"Yes, Jack Savage."

"He's supposed to be in the Crypt."

"We've already seen some people can change that when we ran into Steiner."

"Well, damn."

"You want to piss off a guy like Savage?"

"Absolutely, I definitely want to piss him off," I said. "I worry more about the kind of person who can get a guy from the Crypt out to do something like this."

"They're connected and they have a lot of money."

"Had. Had a lot of money. They just don't know it yet."

"These are bigger fish than we usually go after. These guys who paid for… well, a dead trucker, have a lot of money. Maybe we should walk away."

"She can't hide from people like these. Not even with the new looks. You'd have to be on her identity all the time. Better to just end it. This may be a whole new level for us but I'm on a whole new level, too. Maybe I need to see just how high that level is."

"I was hoping you would have time to figure that out before doing something crazy. And you can't shift."

"We know what level Savage works at. We just need to see what strength level I am working at. As long as it's high enough I'll be fine. One of the best ways to tear it down is to beat them at their own game. Then we drag it all out into the light."

"And you're out in the light again too. You'll be on the news for the third time this year. Are you trying to get caught?"

"I can disappear after this. This is human trafficking just as much as the ring we took down in New York."

"Even more so."

"Can you kill all their digital assets?"

"They'll have physical assets too."

"I'll get those while I'm inside."

"You'll be busy," he said. "I can burn that too. I've found traveling to be a lot easier now. You just make this fight look good since I'm guessing you won't reconsider leaving."

"You *should* leave," Ginger said from the bathroom door. "I can run if I need to. They plan to kill me for sure now. Savage? That bastard is a monster. I see why they never told me the guy's real name. The Crypt is even better than dead."

"No." I stood from the bed and picked up her bag. "You mind if I use some of your clothes?"

"Go ahead. You should listen to your friend."

"I should do a lot of things," I said.

She shook her head and stepped back into the bathroom.

"You're not allowed to stop anywhere else on your way north after this."

"I have to see Deadre."

He sighed. "This place is going to be hot. I saw what was left at the motel in Kentucky. They haven't identified the guy embedded in the truck but I'm guessing it's one of the Talents from Portland?"

"Yeah, the necromancer guy."

"Their leader's brother?"

"Unreasonable people make life so difficult."

"You know they'll be after you with a vengeance."

"I expect so. I'm probably going to have to take care of that at some point. I need to get to where I can shift before I do though."

"Then skip your visit with your ex and go north as soon as this is finished. I say go now but you already set your stubborn-assed mind on this. If we're going to do it, we might as well do it right. There's still a week until the fight. You get your ass figured out and I'll start a deep dive into the finances of these people."

"Don't let some B-rated hacker poof you this time."

"It's a spoof and I'm not living that one down, am I?" He grimaced. "For your information, I seem to remember telling you there are five or six guys like me out there and he was one of them."

"Was he?"

"He most certainly was. Now he's not."

"You seem to have gotten pretty vindictive in your old age."

"Old age? Don't you talk to me about old age, fossil. You were old as dirt when I was born."

"Then you should respect your elders."

"I will when he stops acting like a horny twenty-five-year-old."

"Where's the fun in that?" I asked.

"Exactly. You'd think a century would make you old and wise. Someone left off the wise part."

"Century?" Ginger asked from the bathroom door.

"That's right," Kelen said. "Honey, you been sleeping with a geriatric."

"Who the hell are you, really?"

"Honey, you don't even want to know," he said.

"A century-old shapeshifter that's been on the news multiple times this year?" she asked as she put it together. "You're *that* guy?"

I shrugged. "I guess you could report it and see if you could get the reward. They don't pay until they catch me though and only if your report is the reason."

"But then where would I be?" she asked. "I'm not the person who turns in a BENT legend."

"Don't say things like that," Kelen said. "His head starts to swell up and he's impossible to deal with for weeks."

"They haven't managed to catch me yet either," I said.

"Mostly because of his magnificent tech department," Kelen said as he stood back up. "Speaking of which, I need to go do some tech superstar stuff and get ready to steal a lot of money."

"I think, maybe, orphanages this time," I said.

"Minus our fee of course," he said with a grin.

"Definitely," I said. "We need to replace two escape plans."

"Two?"

"Yeah. The one we gave Bets and the one we're giving Ginger." I looked at her standing in the bathroom door with a towel wrapped around her. "You look like you would like Scotland."

"What?"

"You ever been to Scotland?"

"No. I've driven all across America and some of Canada but nothing overseas."

"There's a nice little cottage and a small farm there waiting for you."

"Of course, now the farm is gone," Kelen grumbled.

She looked at him with a shocked expression and he grinned. He enjoyed this as much as I did. He loved giving them their second chance even as he pissed and moaned about it.

"Too rainy for me anyway," I said. "Now you two can hash out the new identity and I'm going to go out and see if I can lift the front of her truck."

"Really? That's like ten tons."

"Gotta start testing somewhere."

"Jesus," she muttered.

# Chapter 32

"**I** need to deliver this load tomorrow while you work out your plans," Ginger said. "Or you're welcome to join me."

"You'd need me to do the delivery, or you'll need to change back into metal you."

"I know I can change back into metal. What if I do and can't change human again?"

"I don't think it works that way, but you don't have to take the chance if I go with you."

"It's something I'll need to do sometime, isn't it?"

"I don't know. That's entirely up to you. When you get out of here, will you want to change back?"

"I don't know," she said. "I'm not strong when I'm like this. Maybe I need to risk it."

"That's up to you. I can deliver the load if you want to wait to make that decision. It's still four days until the fight and I have time to go do it. Besides, I might get bored hiding inside while you're out. There doesn't need to be two of you out there at the same time. That could cause you troubles later. If they don't believe I'm you, they might come looking for the real you. I doubt they'd break one of Kel's identities but some of the people behind this have resources we won't be able to take, and I would prefer if they had no reason to look."

"I would almost just leave it."

"Would you leave it if I hadn't shown up?"

"No."

"Then we can't leave it now. After this fight, you can disappear but not before."

"Gotta act normal," she said.

"Yep."

"Then let's go deliver in Milwaukee and drop the trailer," she said. "We can bobtail back down here and get this over with."

"It sounds like a plan."

"I'm glad the bumper didn't come off when you lifted the front of my truck. I guess the big bend in it isn't going to hurt anything. I never would have thought you could lift it."

"Could have done more but the bumper would have ripped off if I tried. I already messed the parking lot up where I was standing when I lifted it. That much weight in that small of a place was hard on the asphalt. Concrete might have held but asphalt won't."

"Two new potholes in Illinois aren't gonna stand out." She laughed. "A hundred new potholes wouldn't stand out."

I followed her out of the motel with her bag in my hand. She climbed in the driver's side of the truck, so I shrugged and went to the passenger side. Anyone who knew her might wonder why she let someone else drive her rig, but it was a small thing. Soon enough, we were driving north along Interstate 90.

"I have a lot of questions," she said.

"I guess you do."

"You're him, right? Lloyd?"

"Yeah."

"They call you the worst domestic terrorist this country has ever seen."

"They do."

"There are certain, I guess you'd call them, back channels in the BENT community that say you're more like a BENT Robin Hood. They say the authorities invented most of your crimes."

"Is there a question in this?"

"Who's right?" she asked.

"Both are right, both are wrong."

"That doesn't help."

"They call me a terrorist because I killed a lot of CIA goons. I killed a lot of CIA goons because they lobotomized forty-six telepaths and killed my brother as I tried to break him out of there."

"Jesus."

"Yeah, I have my doubts about whether they got to meet Jesus. I certainly arranged the opportunity."

"And then you went on the run?"

"Been hiding from the CIA since '58."

"Wow."

"Every so often I find a place where I can stay for a while, but sooner or later, I have to move on."

"It sounds awful," she said.

"You know the same lifestyle. You always travel because you can't have a normal life with most people."

"And now I can."

"Yep, every now and then I get to help someone. This new thing with the asteroid chunk is complicated. But if I didn't have it, I would have just been another guy hitching a ride. I couldn't do what I am doing here. Sure, I could have sent you out with a new identity, but tearing down this bunch would have been out of my league."

"Why are you doing it?"

"Because I can."

"Even with all the restriction by not being able to shift?"

"When I get rid of all this mass, I'm not at super strength anymore. I'll use it while I have it."

"Can't you absorb mass again to be stronger?"

"Probably. But, like your testing of the change from metal to flesh, it's all new to me. Maybe I can, maybe it's a one-shot. I won't know until I get to where I can do it. Until then, I'll use the boosted strength for what I do best. Taking down bad people. Those fuckers back there in Rockford are as bad as any of the ones we've taken out before. They're just connected at a level I wouldn't have been able to get to before. Believe me, if this is something I can use freely after I get this damn rock out of me, there's going to be hell to pay for a lot of people I couldn't reach before."

"You should be going to Scotland and disappearing instead of me," she said.

"I'm not ready to disappear yet. Some people need what's coming to them. I intend to bring it to their doorstep."

"Considering what you are rumored to have already done, that should leave a lot of people terrified."

"The key is to do the job without them ever knowing what happened. Rumors only cover a small part of what I've done. Even more since finding Kel. He's a damn wizard. That shit he does inside of computers is straight-up magic."

"I've never seen anything like what he can do," she said.

"No one has."

# Chapter 33

"Looks like we got a ten-eighty-nine at mile marker forty-two. Both lanes are down."

"Shit," Ginger said as the voice spoke on her CB. "Not going back the same way we came up."

"Ten-eighty-nine?" I asked.

"Couple of BENT scrapping in the road. If they have both sides shut down, it must be rough."

"Truckers have a code for that?"

"We have a code for a lot of things."

"You get a lot of these ten-eighty-nines out here on the road?"

"More than you'd think. There are a lot less in the cities, but they still scrap out away from them. Usually, they leave a broken guardrail or something and traffic has to slow down to get through. Both lanes being down could be a lot worse."

"Talents."

"Probably. When the Talents butt heads there's a lot more damage." She shifted down and turned the blinker on. "We'll get off here and go down through Chicago instead."

"How often do you see the same car behind you in this job?"

"What do you mean?"

"I've seen the same car behind us four times now," I said. "Just wondering if it's weird for a trucker. It would be weird for me anywhere else."

"Not too odd for interstate travel. Unless one was before we stopped and dropped the load."

"It's possible. I didn't notice the recurrence until after the drop."

"I was going to ask why it would matter but, considering who you are, I can figure it out. Want me to take the next exit or keep going?"

"Exit."

The black sedan drove on past as we headed down the off-ramp.

"Guess I'm just paranoid."

"You've got a pretty good reason to be. New York is still all messed up after that thing you did a couple of months ago. That really was you, wasn't it?"

"I hate human trafficking."

"What else do you go after? Drug dealers?"

"Nah, I've been known to partake of several illegal substances. I don't like the big Cartels and their way of doing business much. I may interfere with some of that at some point. Most of the bad ones are into human trafficking so they get lumped in with the others."

"What got you after the traffickers?"

"People aren't property. Ever."

"I can agree with that."

"When they decided it was their right to round up telepaths and lobotomize them, I decided they had to go. There are levels of our government that are unaware of the sort of thing other parts are up to. I like to drag it all out in the open now and see if they're worth a damn. The thing with the rock is about to make headlines. We'll see if the so-called good ones step up."

"What happened there?"

"They were experimenting on regular people first. The rock killed them. Fifty or so times they tried it."

"Fifty?"

"Forty-nine to be exact. They used homeless people and addicts."

"Shit," she muttered.

"Then they started trying BENTs. It amplified them but the guy behind it gassed them and killed them all." I stared out the window. "The last one I saw in the videos was a short-distance teleporter who could do line-of-sight teleports. He vanished. Turns out he can teleport anywhere in the world now. I met him recently and he claims to be my son."

"What?"

"Me and Deadre had a thing back in college and she told her boy I was the father. I never even knew. That's why I came through here on my way up north. I have to talk to her."

"And you put all that on hold for me?"

"These fight ring guys are as bad as any human trafficking ring I've ever seen. They were planning to kill you on screen for a bunch of rich perverts. Who knows what else was planned? They need to go down."

"What else?"

"You're a beautiful woman and these guys were already looking for you to die on screen. Kel wouldn't elaborate much on what they were paying for. He said 'snuff film' and I've heard of those before. Most involve sex if you can call it that. Savage has a history along those lines."

"Jesus."

"You hadn't put that together," I said. "I'm sorry. I'm used to the world of trafficking and it's always about sex and power. They may not plan anything like that but if I find out they did, I'm gonna do more than burn it down. Probably going to be a brand new terrorist act all over the news."

"Terrorist act?"

"Yeah, that's what they call it when I kill a bunch of scum. When a superhero does it, it's looked at differently. Deep blue hero shit. When I do it, domestic terrorist. Oh well, it is what it is. They can't want to kill me any more than they already do. I only kill the ones that deserve it."

She swallowed.

"What?" I asked.

"I've been all over the country and seen a lot of bad places, but you talk about killing a lot of people with an ease that makes me nervous."

"It's never easy. You take a life, you take everything they are or ever will be. Any chance at redemption or a future. Some things are beyond redemption. Some people don't deserve redemption or a future." I turned to stare out the window again.

She was quiet as we drove back up the ramp to the interstate.

"You're justifiably upset with it. Most people never have to see things like this. You don't need to be a part of it anymore. Kel has your ID, and you can be on the next plane out. Leave your truck in Chicago and leave this place before it gets ugly. I'll drive it back to Rockford and get this thing done."

"I should be there to help…"

"No, you shouldn't. Get on a plane and fly away knowing there won't be anyone following you."

"How did I deserve any of this? Why are you saving me from a situation I made for myself? I started fighting long before they decided to blackmail me."

"Some people *do* deserve the chance at redemption and a future. Some deserve me."

# Chapter 34

"The sedan's back," I said.

"Are you sure?"

"Same car. I'm used to watching for tails, but these guys are pretty good. They drove right by as we hit that off-ramp. I never saw them again until here. Wonder if they're tracking me or you."

"I don't know," Ginger said.

I picked up her cell phone and called Kelen.

"Admit it. You miss me," he said.

"Hard to miss you when you dress like you do."

"You cut me deep. What can I do for you today, besides contact a tailor? Flannel? Really?"

"Those are *my* clothes," Ginger said.

"No offense, but flannel?"

"I didn't call about the wardrobe," I said.

"You're the one that brought it up."

Ginger chuckled. "He's right."

"Shit," I said. "Anyway, there's a tail behind us in a black sedan. Any way you can check and see who they are?"

"Just a minute."

The phone was silent for a few seconds.

"Driver is Taylor Gleeson with a Portland, Oregon address with the DMV. The other is another Portlander, Jack Linder. They're driving a rental paid for by a Portland—"

"They're mine," I said. "We need Ginger on a plane out of here as we go through Chicago. You have her papers ready?"

"They're just waiting for her to say so."

I looked at Ginger in the driver's seat. She nodded.

"Word's given. I'll get her to O'Hare as soon as you zap that car. I need them to lose sight of the truck for long enough to leave her there."

"No problem. Just say when."

"It's still several miles to the airport. As soon as we reach that exit, you zap it. Then I'll get back on the interstate after dropping her off. You got any idea how they're tracking me?"

"I'm digging deeper, and it looks like Linder is one of those guys that can track anybody. As long as they have something of yours, he can track you."

"Fuck."

"Yep."

"At least they'll follow me after Ginger gets out."

"Sweetie, you need to get the hell out of Chicago. Forget all of this. We can come back and clean it all up then."

"Can't leave yet."

"Just looked deeper into Gleeson. That's not his real name, he's a Talent. He spent a lot of time in one of those silly spandex costumes in the '90s. Larry Drez, also known as Primal."

"I remember that guy. Super strength and healing ability. I thought he was in the Crypt."

"He's supposed to be. He's bad news, Alex."

"He's with a finder. I'm not getting away from them anyway. I'd like to drop Ginger and get out of town before tangling with them, though."

"Agreed."

"Alright, zap 'em," I said as Ginger took the exit.

I smiled as the running lights on the sedan flared brightly and went out. The car made it halfway down the ramp before coming to a stop.

"Go left here and we'll get you to a stop," I said. "Buy a new phone as soon as you get where you can, and Kel will give you instructions from there. I'll lead these guys away."

"I don't even know what to say."

"You don't need to say anything. Just go live a normal life."

After we stopped, I handed her two thousand dollars as she opened the door. "Just use cash until you're back in contact with Kel. Then he'll get you set up. Now, go so I can get moving before those guys show up."

She showed a lot of courage as she walked away from everything she was on the word of America's most wanted terrorist. She would be okay as soon as I got some distance from her so the fallout from whatever was coming wouldn't land on her.

"You never could resist a damsel in distress," Kelen's voice came from the radio.

"Even when they're made of steel and can lift a truck," I said.

"I'll get her out of the area. You get the hell out of Chicago before those two catch up. You sure as hell don't need to scrap with Primal in the city."

"I'm moving," I said and put the truck in gear. "Just need half an hour to get out of the city."

I didn't get my half hour. I didn't even make it back to the interstate before seeing Larry Drez step out into the road in front of me.

"Fuck."

I hit him with the truck.

# Chapter 35

I'd spent a lot of years avoiding the very thing I was about to have to do. I never was a super strength Talent, and I avoided this sort of thing. So, I jumped out of the truck that was somewhat wrapped around Drez and ran. All I could think to do was get out of the city. The last thing I needed was to kill a bunch of innocents in a fight.

Even more paramount was the need for a place to shift. If I did this, it was going to be recorded. I didn't need it to be while wearing the body of Ginger Tucker.

I still hadn't checked what my new mass could do yet other than lift the front of a semi. It turned out that the density of the muscles made for a powerful sprint.

The fastest way out of town would be west, past the airport and I hit the ground running. I had lived around Chicago for a time, but it had been over thirty years ago. There were a lot of changes, and it was like a new city to me.

Just past the airport, there was a large reservoir or retention pond.

"Bingo."

I dove into the center and sank out of sight. Then I shifted. I needed to be as far from "Ginger" as I could. There didn't need to be any mistakes. I came out the other side pulling the remnants of her clothes off. The new ability to form my own "clothing" was nice. I spent a lot less time naked or wearing ill-fitting clothes. I had given myself a pair of jeans and a tank top, shifting into one of the movie stars I enjoyed watching. There weren't as many of them that I liked these days, but I enjoyed Kurt's old movie about a trucker in China town.

I slipped into the alley between two warehouses. The whole area was industrial for a good ways until it hit suburbia. I ran out of the alley and sprinted up Pratt Boulevard.

I felt the vibration as something impacted in the middle of the street in front of me. Drez was standing there holding the other guy in his arms about twenty feet in front of me. I slid to a stop.

"Honeymoon?" I asked.

Drez looked confused for a moment before looking down at the guy in his arms. He set the finder down and pushed him aside.

"I think you've gone far enough, Mister Lloyd. Give me the stone and I'll make it quick and painless."

"As I tried to tell the previous guys, I can't. I don't have it."

"Then long and painful it's going to be."

"Why are you guys all the same? I tried to explain it to the last guys, and they wouldn't listen."

"The stone is secondary. You killed the boss's brother."

"He wanted to kill me and interrogate my corpse. I have a problem with that."

"I'll admit the guy was creepy as shit, but he was still the boss's brother. He sends *me* when things are supposed to be ugly."

"Do you mind if we move it out of town?"

"Funny."

"So that's a no?"

"America's most wanted terrorist is worried about casualties?"

"I only kill people who deserve it." I looked at Linder. "Or the people who lead the ones who deserve it to me."

Linder took a step back.

"Don't worry, Jack," Drez said. "He's not going to be killing anyone anymore. Never killed a shifter before. I think I'll tear you into little pieces and send you to the CIA in a hundred little packages. Collect my reward."

"Good luck with that," I said.

"You're not dealing with someone like Halleck," he said and strode toward me.

"I'm not exactly the same shifter either."

I looked for a way out but there wasn't one. So, I stepped forward and met his incoming fist with a raised elbow. I'd seen the move in a fight between a couple of bare-knuckle fighters. The spot just below the elbow is a hard surface if it's held in the right position and will damage someone's fist, possibly breaking the wrist.

Unless they have super strength and are close to indestructible. Then it becomes the unstoppable force meeting the immovable object and the shock wave shatters glass up and down the street. It also happens to turn the brain of a certain "Finder" to mush. Linder collapsed with blood spewing from his ears.

I staggered backward but he had made no headway either.

"Not the same shifter at all," I said.

He looked at Linder and shrugged. "This might be a lot more fun than I expected. I haven't had a good fight since Detroit."

"We should take this out of town," I said, looking at the shattered glass along the street.

Traffic was nonexistent as people ran from their cars. Luckily, no one else had been close enough to get the same treatment that Linder had received.

"Did you see that fight in Detroit?"

"Yeah, the whole country did. You and Kline took out three city blocks and killed fourteen people."

"I thought it was more," he said and charged toward me.

I stepped into his charge, but he was expecting it and grabbed my left arm. He swung me in an arc and threw me back toward the airport.

"Fuck," I said as I sailed, spinning through the air.

There was a row of planes at what I expected was a maintenance area and he had hurled me right at it. There wasn't much I could do without shifting and I couldn't risk Drez getting a boost like that. So, I clipped the tail of the closest jet in the row and slammed into the concrete below.

"This has to stop," I said and staggered out from under the wreckage that had fallen on top of me.

I saw a shadow just before he landed and hit me again, sending me crashing through two more of the parked jets.

At least we were in the maintenance area. If they had been loaded with people, there would have been casualties.

He jumped from where he was before he hit me and landed right beside me again. Grabbing my arm, he spun in another circle and threw me toward the terminal. There would be people there.

I landed just short of the building and rolled to my feet to find myself staring at the large glass building and hundreds of faces.

Drez landed right behind me. "Now the fun starts. I can do this all day."

He reached for me, and I rolled left and hooked my left arm around his left arm, pulling him closer. Then my right went under his right pulling him into a Full Nelson.

He tensed and it was like holding a solid object.

"This is your last chance," I said, straining to hold him. "Stop. Don't make me kill you."

"Kill me? You can barely hold me. I can jump us right through that building."

I felt him tense to jump and I did the only thing I could think of. I wasn't sure how I had triggered it before, but I willed myself to have more mass and Drez screamed. My arms fell out of the Nelson because there wasn't anything to hold. Both arms and a good-sized part of his torso were gone. This time I saw how it worked. It was like it dissolved into its base molecules and flowed into me.

He stopped screaming as the process reached his chest. I stopped the absorption and found myself standing in a small crater where I had pulled mass from the concrete below me too.

Turning around, I found hundreds of people staring out the windows of the terminal. Many were holding their phones up and recording.

"Fuck."

# Chapter 36

I tried to step away from the terminal and stumbled with the added strength.

"Shit."

I looked up to see a news chopper incoming, but I couldn't trust a run yet, so I did the same thing Drez had done. I jumped west toward the warehouses again. I needed to get out of sight and shift again. If there was one news chopper there would be more, they would be all over the place. They would flood the area like locusts. It wouldn't take long, and this new face would be plastered on every TV in the nation.

I landed next to a warehouse and staggered into the alley alongside. Looking around, it seemed to be unused. I stepped deeper into the alley and still covered more space than I wanted. Stopping next to a dumpster, I placed a hand out to steady myself. It crushed the lip of the steel container.

"Damn."

I shifted back into Ginger, trying not to lose any mass.

The fine red dust still floated in the air around me.

I guess I was leaving a little gift in Chicago after all.

I slowly walked out of the alley in the woman's form, wearing jeans and a flannel shirt. Concentration kept my stride down to a normal speed. Drez had been a lot of mass in a compact area, and I had absorbed about a quarter of that mass before stopping. It would take some time to adapt. Hopefully, I had enough time to adapt to it before the match in three days.

I walked right out in the open as the news choppers started closing in. They were looking for a guy that looked a lot like a movie star, not a woman made of living metal. I was getting the hang of holding that normal speed after about three blocks.

Flagging down a cab, I slipped into the back seat and the car settled a lot.

"No. No. Too much weight." The cabbie shook his finger at me, and I got back out. His English wasn't great, but I could understand him well enough. "I will call cousin, you stay here. Ten minutes."

"Alright."

I could see his dilemma. I weighed twelve hundred pounds and Drez had probably weighed the same. I took on about a quarter of his mass plus that divot of concrete. I was probably a ton by now. Too much for the back seat of a car.

He was right. Ten minutes later a tow truck stopped in front of me.

The driver-side window opened and another middle-eastern man looked out. "Aziz said you need a tow truck. Where is your car?"

His English was much better than his cousin's.

"It's not for a car. I need to go to Rockford. I weigh too much for his cab."

He chuckled. "A smart man will never ask a woman's weight."

"Close to a ton," I said.

"Then you definitely need to ride in the truck."

I very carefully climbed into the passenger seat which sank all the way down. It had a similar design to the seats in Ginger's truck.

"You get some heavy passengers?"

"Aziz calls me when there is a car to tow or a person who has a heavy Bend. I had the seat special ordered just for such occasions."

"Nice. It's good that I ran into Aziz."

"Any of the cab drivers in the area call me," He said as he put the truck in gear. "Several are my cousins. My name is Asher. Rockford is a little further than my normal fare."

"If you can stop by a phone, I'll see to it you're paid."

"You have no phone?"

"I break them too easily. A payphone would be great."

"Easy enough," he said. "There are only a few of them."

"It is unknown who the mystery Talent was during the attack at O'Hare Airport this afternoon," the reporter said. "But it has been verified that the dead Talent was Larry Drez, also known as Primal. Drez was believed to be incarcerated in the superhuman prison known as the Crypt. Investigations are rumored to be in the works. There were two confirmed fatalities and many injuries due to the concussive force from their initial contact."

The reporter motioned toward the road to her left. "It looks like this has become a bit more serious as the black SUVs arrive. This usually means the CIA is getting involved."

She motioned for the camera to follow and hurried toward the new arrivals as they exited their vehicles. They wore the customary black suits and looked like a football team.

"Does the CIA involvement mean the mystery Talent is not a mystery?"

The agent frowned and pointed back the way she had come.

"Is it true that Kurt Russell is a Talent and is here in Chicago?"

He stepped toward her with an open-air of menace.

"Fine. Fine. We'll just let the footage speak for itself."

The TV went to static and then a picture of Kelen's face replaced the broadcast.

"What the hell was that? I can't leave you alone for a damned minute."

"Drez didn't like the stalled car. He followed on foot. I managed to get away."

"Oh, I saw that. You absorbed a big chunk of the guy on video, looking like a movie star, no less.

The public might not know the new you, but you can bet the CIA recognized that stunt."

"They're already at the airport."

"Honey, you need to get out of there," he said. "Forget this fight. Just leave."

"They'll start hunting her if I leave."

"They're already hunting *you*."

"It's only two more days. Then I can go see Deadre and get out of here."

"You want to go back to Chicago?"

"It's what I came here for."

"Are you stupid?"

"Sometimes."

"What possible purpose would there be to that?"

"I need to know."

"We can find out later," he said. "Hell, I can connect you to her personal phone from here."

"Alright," I said. "After the fight and we take down this ring, I'll go north. Once I get this damn rock out of me, I'll come back to see her. I have to do this face to face."

"That's probably the first smart decision you've made in a year," he said with obvious relief in his voice.

"I see how it's gonna be."

"Everything since New York has been just one screw-up after another."

"Maybe I should have gone with Twilight."

"I've been trying to get you to retire for years. Do it. Go lay on a beach. Climb a mountain. Do something besides run around chased by the CIA."

"Where's the fun in that?"

"You're crazy, old man."

"Don't go rushing to judgment on that."

"I've known you for thirty-three years. There was no rush in the judgment. You get crazier the older you get."

"I've been feeling the years, kid." I stood up and the bed creaked. "But in all honesty, now it feels like it did when I was in my twenties. If this stupid dust wasn't changing people, I would be having a blast."

"Like I said, crazy."

"Maybe." I cautiously stepped forward toward the bathroom. "I really don't understand how guys like Drez and the other super-strength guys can even function like regular people. I was barely maintaining a normal pace with it before this jump."

"It takes most people years to adapt to their strength and it doesn't change. We have to get you somewhere so you can safely drop that mass."

"Soon, kid. Soon. Did Ginger get out of Chicago?"

"Yes. She's safely on a plane to Scotland."

"Good. I think I might have freaked her out a little."

"I can say that for certain," he said. "She felt like she should stay but the woman is terrified."

"I was a little too… well, me."

"It happens."

"That's what I liked about Twilight. She didn't even blink."

"It's not that common," he said.

"Agreed," I said. "Now go away. I have to try to use this bathroom without breaking anything."

"Good luck," he said and laughed.

# Chapter 37

Kelen was undoubtedly right, and I knew I should get the hell out of there. But I knew they would hunt for the girl if I did. I wasn't sure they wouldn't go looking anyway but after Kelen was through with them they wouldn't be in any shape to do anything. In my experience, the people who paid for something like this would be after the one they paid, not the intended victim.

What I had told him was true. I didn't feel the age creeping up on me like I did before. Then, it took a lot of my concentration to keep from falling apart. Now I was concentrating just to keep from hurting everyone around me. I was having the time of my life and almost hated to see it go. When I got rid of the rock would I still have the new abilities? I thought so. Adam could still long-distance teleport. He said it was a one and done type of thing. The rock could only affect me the one time... I hoped.

I had two days to get ready for the fight with Savage and I needed to relearn what my body could do so I put on some of Ginger's clothes and left the room. Trekking into the farmland that surrounded Rockford, I started exploring what I could do. Running through cornfields to get used to my speed and strength seemed the easiest way to get a handle on what I was dealing with.

I found a huge field and started running down a long row. I wasn't interested in destroying a farmer's crops, so I ran to the end of the row and turned to run down the next. I zig-zagged through that cornfield for several hours before slowing the pace to a normal person's speed.

It's tough to slow your life down to blend in with others. I'd never had too much trouble with it when I was a three-hundred-pound man in a smaller body. But now I weighed in close to a ton and still in a small body. It was fighting one's self the whole way. How did the super-strength talents manage to do it? I was struggling the whole time.

Kelen's statement was probably accurate. They learn in years what I was trying to grasp in weeks or days. I didn't expect the fight with Savage to be difficult to win, it would be difficult to make it look good while I did it. He had been the same strength for decades. I was eight hours into this one. The problem would be letting him throw me around while all the bets were placed. It might not even be possible to fool Savage once he realized how much I weighed.

Unless he was an idiot. There was always the chance he was. Of course, Ginger had informed me that she and Savage had never met so there was a chance he wouldn't realize what he was up against.

Maybe I shouldn't even worry about putting on a show. The closer the time came to fight, the angrier I got. The whole situation was disgusting to me. I had been taking down human traffickers for years in various places and this was no less. The fighting ring was enough to tear it down but this latest step in their game was much worse. The people behind this whole thing needed to be stopped. And Savage… well, he deserved little pity after the things he'd done.

Springing someone like Savage out of the Crypt to kill Ginger on screen for rich perverts was enough to make my blood boil. This was so far over the line I couldn't even build up any pity for those behind it.

Frankly, I wondered how one of the major Talents hadn't found out about it and squashed it. I could imagine someone like Saberhagen hitting something like this. He was as close to a god as one of us could get. Super strength, invulnerability, flying and God only knows what else the guy could do. The strength and invulnerability could be explained by body density which I was very aware of but the flying while being that heavy baffled me. I like to have an explanation for how things work and that one, I did not. Perhaps it was a form of telekinesis.

I understood Twilight. Her wings were large enough to carry her. She weighed a little over a hundred pounds. When I did a flying shift, I had to put so much into my wings that my body became ultra-light. I couldn't even imagine what size wings I would need to carry the ton I weighed.

The whole thing would be simpler if I just sent word to someone like Saberhagen about what was happening or to the authorities in Rockford or Chicago. But what fun would that be? These people would fade into the darkness and Savage would go back to the Crypt. I think not, he wasn't going back.

This newfound strength had its uses, even if it was a bitch to get used to. It relied on a great deal of focus to use it right. If your density had you moving at a much faster rate, your mind had to be able to operate at that rate as well or there's no telling what sort of mess you could get into. Like running into the tree at the end of the sixteenth row of corn on a farm in Illinois. The tree doesn't fare all too well when a ton hits it at high speed.

"So much for not damaging anything," I muttered as I extricated myself from the fallen tree.

# Chapter 38

I managed to stay out of trouble for the two days until fight night. I dug in her bag and found the form-fitting suit Ginger wore to fight. The girl was proud of what she had and wore the clothes to show it off. Of course, that was part of the show, though. It was the same when you were in a gym. They were proud of their bodies and liked to show it.

"She had enough of a narcissistic streak to bump uglies with a woman who looked just like her." I chuckled

Donning jeans and a flannel over the body suit, I exited the motel. Surprisingly no one had called on her cell to see if she had survived the crash of her truck in Chicago. She had lived a solitary life it seemed. They mentioned casualties on the news report but not her name or anything about her.

I wondered if she would actually get to live a life after this. Regardless, it was better than what Savage had in store for her. After Baltimore, I didn't have much doubt about what was planned. Savage deserved—

"Honey, we have to *leave*." Kelen interrupted my thoughts.

He was standing right beside me after stepping from an alcove to my right.

"I know," I said. "I'm on my way."

"No, we need to leave. The CIA is crawling all over Chicago they're bringing in the big guns. They have Null with them."

"I'm not worried about Null. He can stop me from shifting but not much more. His power is mental and won't affect body density. Billy knows better than to come at me after the last time, anyway."

"Null can stop *me*, sweetie."

"Then I think you should get out of here. Better yet, send Billy a message. Tell him that I have a strength talent now that he can't affect. Tell him if he shows, I will rip his little pin head off. After that bull shit in Florida, he deserves it. I don't want to kill him, and he doesn't want to be dead."

"Really?"

"Yes."

"I don't get it," he said and laid a hand on my shoulder. "What's going on here? We've bugged out for a lot less. The girl is safe. They're not getting past my background for her. You're okay with coming back to see Deadre later. What's left? We can come after these guys anytime."

"If Null stays after the warning, I'll go. I can't risk your life for this. But if he goes, I'm going to finish this. He can't be able to do it again."

"Who?" Kelen stopped. "Savage?"

I was silent.

"This isn't about the girl, the money, or the pervs. You want *him*."

"This may be my only chance to get to him. I do want their money, I want the pervs, and I want the girl safe. But what I really want is to be in a room with that son of a bitch while I can do this."

I squeezed a steel post as we walked past, and it crushed under my hand.

"Then we go in hard," Kelen said. "Don't worry about making things look good. Get the job finished and we go. I'll hit them fast and dirty. You do what you need to."

"You're not even going to ask why?"

"Honey, I know *you*. If you want this that badly, he did something pretty awful. Considering who we're talking about, I'm not sure I want to know the details. His stay in the Crypt, courtesy of Saberhagen, included charges of terrorism, rape, murder, robbery, and a stack of papers listing all of the other felonies. I don't want to know, but now I want to forget the finesse, and just blitz this one."

"Blitz is fine," I said. "Send the message to Null. If he doesn't take the warning seriously, I want you to get the hell out of here and let me deal with it."

"Most of your escape plans need my help."

"Which you can do from a distance."

"I still think you're crazy, old man."

"Probably."

"Then hurry your pretty ass up and go hurt that bastard." He stepped into another alcove where I could see a city power box.

I grinned and walked around the corner, approaching the large building where the fight would occur. It was about five stories, and I was a little worried about containment. Two talents duking it out inside a building in the middle of town didn't seem very smart.

Ginger said something about a ring made for that, but I didn't get as much information as I wished before the idiots from Portland showed up. I figured I would play it by ear. That was part of what made my job fun. There was a lot more planning in my later years, but this felt like something I would do in my thirties. I got into a lot of trouble in my younger years.

I stepped inside the building to find a large Latino waiting just inside the door.

"Ah, chica, we been waiting for you."

"Rico," I said in greeting.

I recognized Rico Santiago. He was a talent that specialized in blades. He created them from his own body and used them quite well. I wondered what kind of diet he had to live on to be able to do that. Santiago was a low-level criminal I had never needed to look into. He was a bruiser for some of the organizations I was familiar with.

"You are in a new room today, chica. Follow me."

"You have any idea who this guy is I'm fighting?"

"You gonna love this guy," he said looking back toward me with a wide grin.

I grimaced as he turned away. It looked like Rico Santiago might have just made my list since he didn't reveal a name.

My list would probably grow a lot today.

I followed Rico up the stairs and down a hallway toward the center of the building. There we entered an elevator and I saw the indicator going down as we began to move. A room very deep underground might contain two Talents as they scrapped. We didn't go near as deep as I expected, and I was again wondering about containment.

"Alright, chica." Rico pointed to a door. "In there is your change room and when you're ready, just go out the other side to the pit."

"Sounds easy enough," I said.

He chuckled. "You got this, chica. You gonna love this one. We got a special clientele today. Lots of money riding on this."

"Yeah, I think I will love it."

He smirked as he turned around.

"Definitely on the list," I muttered and opened the door.

# Chapter 39

"Figures," I said as I stepped through the door, and it slammed closed behind me.

The room I was in was definitely not a changing room. It was over a hundred feet across in both directions. I wasn't even sure how it fit inside the building. This must have been what Ginger was talking about. A special room made for this kind of fight. There was not going to be a changing room. They weren't taking any chances. There would be no chance for me to have second thoughts and back out.

It also was nothing like the fight room Ginger had described. This would have been an utter surprise when she walked into it. A door in the far wall opened and a large man walked through. I doubted that he could see the feral grin plastered on my face.

"Now this is what I'm talking about," I muttered.

I didn't bother removing the jeans and flannel as I strode forward to meet Savage.

"Ginger, Ginger," a voice filled the room. "Someone told me you wanted to leave us. Tonight you'll have that chance, my dear. Tonight, one of you in that room will leave and be free to do as you will. The other will never leave. There's no way out of here except my way. Victory or death."

I kept walking toward Savage.

"Your opponent tonight is undefeated here in the Circle of Power. Now is your chance to attempt to change that. Of course, that might be difficult since the man you face is Jack Savage, the Bonecrusher!"

This is what they'd been waiting for, the realization to sink in that I was doomed. I was sure there was a camera zoomed in on me to see my terror. I was grinning with excitement. I was pretty sure that wasn't what they expected from Ginger Tucker. Frankly, I didn't care.

Ten years I had dreamed of being able to confront this bastard. Only in dreams was I able to do anything about him.

We stopped about ten feet apart.

He smirked as he looked up and down my body. "Damn, this is gonna be fun."

I raised an eyebrow. "I'm going to do something for you that hurts me to my very soul. I'm going to give you one opportunity to turn around and walk away."

He laughed. "Or what?"

"There's only one reason I'm standing here in this weird assed room." I pointed toward him. "Do you remember Donna DeMarco?"

"Who the fuck is that?"

"Donna DeMarco was a nineteen-year-old girl that stepped in and protected some folks in Baltimore during an armed robbery. It was ten years ago, a little before Saberhagen caught up to you."

"Oh, hell! I *do* remember her. God, that girl was a firecracker."

"There aren't many who know what you did to her after you dragged her down the street. She was a sweet kid, and you broke her. When she killed herself the next month it broke her mother's heart."

He leered.

"The DeMarcos were my friends and I never even dreamed I would actually get to be in the same room with you. Now is the moment to make your decision. Walk away."

"Walk away? You have no idea what's in store for you. What I did to that DeMarco chick pales to what I'm about to do to you. They say you're strong. You're gonna need all that durability to handle me. I did Demarco hard but I'm gonna take my time with you." He raised his fist in front of his face and turned it a few times. "I'm gonna stick my fist—"

I hit him. I crossed the ten feet between us before he could even move. Pulling my punch at the last minute, he still flew back to slam into the wall fifty feet behind him with a resounding thud. I was a little surprised at the strength of the wall.

I walked forward as Savage staggered to his feet.

"Someone lied," he said as he straightened up. He beat on the wall.

"They told you the truth they knew. You thought I was going to be someone trapped in here with you. But you're trapped in here with me and I don't think they're going to let you out."

He was rubbing his chest where I had punched him.

"Did you know that someone like us who has broken bones has to go to a specialist? We have to use a doctor with as much strength as ourselves to be able to set the bones." I stepped closer. "Found that out in med school. See, they have to have the strength to push the break back into place."

He pounded on the wall again. "Let me out! Damn you!"

"I already gave you the chance to walk away. You don't get another."

He turned and threw a punch.

I caught it in my hand and the sound from the collision boomed inside of the room.

"When you raped my friend's daughter, I thought of the perfect punishment. I've dreamed for years of being able to exact it. I plan to hurt you, Jack Savage. Saberhagen should have done it long ago, but you surrendered without resisting. He's too nice. He thought the authorities would punish you. Out in the real world, there's always someone stronger, but inside? Inside, you were the top dog."

"I surrender," he said. "Take me back to the Crypt."

"He's too nice. I'm not."

I hit him again and he slammed into the wall once more.

"I'm going to break you, Jack Savage. I'm going to break your bones. I think I'll do it in alphabetical order." I grabbed one of his arms and pulled him forward. "Some think the capitate bone comes first, that's the one right here in the wrist." I put pressure on his wrist, and he screamed. I yanked him forward and slammed him to the ground. "But the first one is the calcaneus bone, commonly referred to as the heel bone."

I yanked his right foot forward and slammed my elbow down on the heel. This time I didn't pull my punch and I felt it crush with the impact.

"Oh, I'm not sure they'll be able to set that one," I said as he screamed under me. "I should probably skip the vertebrae for now and move along. You think this is what Donna felt as you threw her around and brutalized her? I hope it didn't hurt her as much, because you're howling a lot and we're just getting started. Let me see those capitate bones now."

# Chapter 40

I didn't make it all the way through the bones before he went into shock, but I got the major ones. I grew tired of it after he cried. I wasn't sure he'd ever felt real pain. Some can't handle it at all, and some have a very high tolerance.

I stood up and scowled at the Bonecrusher.

"That was well deserved but not as satisfying as it should have been," I said. "Open the door."

The walls closed in and stopped at about ten feet from me. A face appeared on the wall I faced. It seemed to be molded from the wall itself.

"I don't think that's gonna be an option," it said. "The boss says to leave it closed."

"I'm going to give you one chance to open the door."

"Ginger dear," the original voice said. "After consulting the patrons of this event, I have come to the conclusion that this was quite unsatisfactory."

"I did too."

"What these patrons paid for was something a little more centered on you, my dear. It seems our champion is not going to be able to provide the entertainment as promised but there is an alternative. Sometimes we have to resort to the old tried and true methods."

"Figures," I said. "The pervs still want a show."

"The room around you is what we commonly refer to as 'The Box' and it's a favorite of certain patrons. The Box is what you could almost call a pocket dimension. Inside the Box, everything is under Darrell's control. Now Darrell has a wonderfully twisted imagination, and the Box is unbreakable. I've decided to let him play and we'll see if we can't come to a satisfactory conclusion."

I turned to my right where the wall had changed. There were tentacles growing from the wall and some ugly-looking furniture growing from the floor.

"Fuck. That's not happening," I said. "Darrell, this is your moment where you make a choice. This is the chance I mentioned. Open the door."

"But this is gonna be so much funner."

"Not sure that's a word. I'm pretty sure that's supposed to be more fun. But, I gave you your chance." I walked to the wall with the face.

"Go ahead," the face said. "Give it a couple of swings. You'll see. It's unbreakable and you have no choice. That's the point of the Box. You are at the mercy of something you can't control and—"

I placed a hand over the mouth and willed for more mass. I expected the wall to dissolve but it didn't exactly do that. It flashed like a strobe light a couple of times as a scream reverberated inside the Box. Then it all just disappeared. I was standing in the center of a stage in a theatre-like room.

At the front of the stage were a pair of chairs facing me. In the one on the left sat a large man in a white suit. His face showed the utter shock he was feeling. Beside him was a man with a scream frozen on his face. Well, the half of his face that remained. Half of his head was just gone.

"Darrell? Are you okay?" I asked.

The big man turned to his partner and started shaking.

I stepped from the stage, and he raised his hand in a placating motion, "Now Ginger, remember what I have. If you touch me, it goes to the authorities."

"What you have is a short future, fat man," I said as I stopped beside him. "Very short."

I put a finger on his sternum and pushed slightly. There was a crack and he lurched as it pierced his heart.

I didn't feel pity for the man, nor for the special clientele of the evening but it didn't look like I was going to get the chance to do more than I had already done. Familiar uniformed troops flooded into the theatre from the rear. The special clientele would have enough to explain to the cops. The CIA was getting smarter. They sent in the locals first and I wasn't going to kill a bunch of cops.

I jumped up with a good deal of force and crashed through the ceilings above, all five of them. I'd used enough force to send me into the open air above the building.

Landing in the parking lot of a neighboring building, I ran west into the night. I was almost out of Rockford when I heard something above me, and someone settled lightly to the ground in front of me.

"Hello there, Mister Lloyd."

"Fuck."

Fucking Saberhagen.

# Chapter 41

Saberhagen was the last person I wanted to see. I'd taken a lot of pains to not be anywhere near New Mexico where he lived.

"I didn't expect to run into you here, Mister Saberhagen. And I really didn't want to do that at all."

"Careful, you'll hurt my feelings. The name is just Saberhagen, by the way. Mister Saberhagen was my father."

"I never expected you to be working with the likes of the CIA. You know they hate us all, don't you?"

"Many people hate us, Mister Lloyd."

"Alex, since we're getting all chummy," I said. "I think we should move this outside of the city if you're planning on getting physical. I don't have any interest in hurting any civilians. I'm not the bad guy here but they probably never explained anything. Why would they let something like the truth get in the way?"

"The fact that you wish to get out of the city before engaging in any sort of conflict earns you a little time for explanations."

I pointed to the west. "I'm going to jump that way."

He nodded and I jumped. The concrete of the sidewalk cracked as I left the ground. I landed in a field outside of Rockford and watched as he floated lightly to the ground.

"It would be nice if I could land like that."

"It is a lot easier on the terrain." He motioned toward the big ditch I had left with my landing.

"I guess we should go on and get down to it," I said. "I can't let you take me in. They'll cut me up into little pieces. I'm possibly the only person on the planet who could take you out, but I'll be damned if I'm the guy that does that. The only way I go is in a box."

He raised an eyebrow. Just looking at the man, you would think he was an average Joe. He wasn't overly tall or rugged and he didn't dress the part of Superman from the old comics. He could be anyone you'd pass in the street without noticing. But he wasn't.

"If I'm correct Mister Lloyd, Alex, you firmly believe you could defeat me, yet you refuse?"

"I do. But the only way it would work involves death and I'm not willing to do that."

"Yet you've killed many people."

"I have," I said. "A couple of them less than ten minutes ago. I believe in redemption. Redemption for those that are redeemable. Some people are a cancer to society, and I believe in removing them. The two men back there, they liked to trap women in a pocket dimension and make their own little snuff films as they rape and kill them."

"I see."

"I kill bad people, I won't deny it. But I won't kill the good guys. I couldn't kill the local cops they sent rushing into that place, and I won't kill the best of us standing here in a field in Illinois. I'll damn sure fight to my last breath before letting the CIA take me."

"I suppose we're both fortunate, then, considering I don't work for the CIA. I'm not here on their behalf nor am I here to apprehend you. I think you know where to find a certain object that was stolen recently."

I couldn't hide my surprise. "You're *not* with those pricks in Portland, are you?"

"I don't think I know anyone in Portland."

"That's at least some relief. Those assholes want me dead."

"That seems to be quite prevalent these days. Chicago looks like someone kicked a hornet nest. But it changes nothing at the moment. Where did you hear about the fragment? And how did you find it? I never even told anyone it existed."

"Wait… what?"

"Someone had to have pulled it from my mind," he said.

"I stole it from a CIA black site where they had killed fifty or so people with it before starting their experiments on BENT."

He stared at me a moment. "You're telling the truth."

"No point in lying now," I said. "Problem is, I ended up touching the damned thing during the heist and amped up my abilities. I can absorb mass now where I was limited to my own before. With Frank Steiner beating on me and needing more strength, my ability did what it needed and absorbed mass. Unfortunately, one of the first things it absorbed was the rock… and Steiner… and about half the room."

"Amazing," he muttered. "Again, you're telling the truth."

"How can you know that?"

"I can hear your heartbeat. Yours is different than a normal person but it still reads the same. I've been detecting lies from my earliest years. So, you aren't the one who found it in Peru?"

"Nope. I got it in Prescott."

"Where exactly is it?"

"You're looking at it. It's part of the ton of mass I'm carrying around. If I shift, it leaves little patches of dust that seem to enhance others. It didn't kill a normal when it happened the first time, but I don't want to take any chances." I stared at him for a moment. "How did you know it was in Peru?"

"Because I hid it there."

"Say what?"

He chuckled. "I wasn't always this strong. In reality, I wanted to write books. I found the fragment in '62, actually, not too far from here. I was working for Motorola and had a low-level strength Bend that I kept to myself mostly. I touched the fragment, and everything changed."

"Damn."

"After seeing what it did to me, I didn't really trust that it would be good to let the authorities get it. So, I used my newfound ability to fly the thing to a remote spot in Peru. A spot I thought would be quite safe. And it was for fifty years."

"Any ideas how the CIA ended up with it?"

"I thought you had found it. It's troublesome to think how they might have gained the knowledge of where it was."

"Think they may have a telepath?"

"I don't know, but I am thinking of looking a little deeper into them."

"That's not a bad thing. I'd have dragged them out into the light if I could have. I may be able to do more in the future with my newfound abilities. That is, if you don't have to kill me."

He grinned. "I'm not a killer Mister… Alex. And you've already established that it would be the only way I could take you in. Therefore, I can't bring you in."

"That's quite a relief."

# Chapter 42

"Damn, you got the whole Superman package," I said as the ice wall in front of us began to melt. "Heat vision?"

"Not exactly. I had a minor telekinesis Bend, and I was a little stronger before touching the fragment. The fragment sparked several other abilities as well as the strength." He stepped to the side. "Might want to move over."

I heard the water and stepped aside before the hole erupted. The melted ice was a fountain for a moment.

"This is a mix of pyro-kinesis and telekinesis. I push the heat through telekinetic lenses and magnify it like the sun through a magnifying glass."

"So, you got heat vision."

He sighed. "I should have just kept writing. Had a great idea about sentient machines, but no, fiction became reality with superpowers. Do you have any idea what the most popular book genre is? The whole 'what if the asteroid never fell?' thing is what everyone wants to see."

"I don't doubt that. I do a lot of wondering about that very thing. I'm fairly certain I wouldn't be at the north freakin pole watching superman melt a hole in the polar ice cap so I can bury this asteroid dust that causes BENT to become Talents so deep it never sees the light of day."

He laughed. "That's a fair assumption."

"You say you liked to write?"

"Yes, I had a plan to publish. It went out the window when the asteroid fell. Well, a couple of years later, anyway."

"I was planning to be a bartender." I shrugged. "I was learning every way you could drink rum."

"Rum?" he laughed again. "I used to love drinking rum."

"I still do," I said. "Although it takes a lot to feel it with all this mass."

"It certainly does. I tried a few years ago when I lost Joan."

"Sorry, man."

"You know what it's like. We're the old guard. You and I were there the day it fell. I don't even know how long it will take me to reach old age. I feel the same as I did the day I found the fragment."

"My shifting would keep me young before, but I could feel the clock ticking. After touching the rock, I feel like I'm twenty again. I have no idea where it's going to lead but I'm kind of itching to find out." I looked into the hole he'd burned in the ice. "You gonna bury me down there?"

"No," he said. "Don't think I haven't thought of it. But, I'm not sure if I could live with myself."

"If I were you, I'd throw me in there and freeze it back up."

"Didn't get the freeze breath."

"Alright then, let's get this done," I said and walked into the tunnel.

I heard his steps behind me and expected the strike to happen at any moment. Me carrying the fragment around was dangerous, but he was true to his word. We reached the end of the tunnel about three hundred yards into the ice.

"Now hold on while I get this ready. Shift if you need to. I've already been changed by it."

I shifted my right arm into a long spike that thrust into the ground.

He looked down and the floor at the end of the tunnel bubbled with the heat.

"Heat vision," I said with a grin.

He stopped and there was a pool where he had melted the ice. Steam filled the end of the tunnel for a few minutes. He spun around faster than I could register, and the steam was blown down the tunnel toward the opening.

"Not bad," I said.

He shrugged as he stopped spinning. "Theoretically you should be able to drop the mass into the pool. How does it work?"

"I have no idea. I've shifted several times but tried not to lose mass. There's always a cloud of red dust. I've never actually tried to expel it before. I guess there's no time like the present."

I shifted from the shape of Ginger Tucker into one I'd used before sparingly. Average height and build with brown eyes and black hair. Not overly handsome but not ugly either. I also wished to lose mass.

The area around me swirled with particles as my body shed excess mass. It was like the red dust I had seen before but much thicker. As it settled around us on the floor, He began pushing it into the pool. A ton of what looked like various colors of sand piled up pretty quick and it displaced the water in the pool which sloshed around us on the floor mixing with the other sand.

"It's a little messy," I said. "It could be worse. It would suck if I had to vomit it all up."

I took a step and it felt weird without having to concentrate to keep myself slowed down. "I was starting to enjoy the super strength." I watched Saberhagen push the last of the sand into the pool. "I guess this would be the time for you to take me in."

"You could still absorb mass and then where would I be?"

"Told you I wouldn't do that. No way do I kill a BENT legend."

"And I told you I'm not interested in apprehending you. I'm not arresting a BENT legend."

I laughed. "I guess I need to test this outside."

To my surprise, we walked out of the tunnel.

He turned and cut a piece of ice from the ice wall and plugged the hole. Then he flew above and melted an ice tunnel down into the other where the water would fill the previous tunnel. Then he began melting the outside until all of it was full of water.

He did something and I watched the water freeze solid.

"I thought you didn't get the freeze breath."

"I didn't. It's part of the joining of pyro—"

"You got freeze breath."

He sighed.

I chuckled and shifted a few times with no dust haze around me. I settled back into the form I had taken in the tunnel.

"I remember the old reports from '58," he said. "That's your original."

"Yep. Before, when I turned back to the original, it was a ninety-three-year-old man. He's not there anymore."

"It looks like expelling the mass took care of your problem," he said. "Can I drop you off anywhere?"

"Anywhere in the states is fine. You know, I'm thinking I might need to run by Portland, now that you mention it."

"I can do that."

"Thanks."

I think he knew I meant it for much more than just giving me a ride.

# Chapter 43

"Where *exactly* the fuck have you been?"

Kelen walked out of the door of an old apartment complex seconds after I dialed the phone.

"It's a little hard to explain."

"No, it's not. Just open your mouth and explain why it's been three days since I heard from you. I finished with that bunch in Rockford and there was no sign of you. I've been hunting through the whole Midwest trying to find word of you. I burned through the CIA's systems three times and nothing."

"As I was clearing the area, I ran into Saberhagen," I said.

He stepped back with a shocked look on his face. "Fuck."

"That's what I said."

"Did you have to…?"

"No. I don't kill legends."

He stared at me for a moment. "Jesus! Spit it out."

"He actually helped me get rid of the rock."

He took a breath. "And you still couldn't call?"

"No towers where we left it. Frankly, I expected to be disappeared while we were there, but it seems he doesn't kill legends either."

"Fucking Saberhagen called you a legend?"

"He did."

"Oh my god, I'll never hear the end of it."

"Probably not. So, what happened in Rockford?"

"You were right about Null. He was on the next plane out of Chicago. So, I went in hard and took down every account that was tied to Darvis Kelly's little club."

"Darvis Kelly?"

"Yeah, the fat guy they found with a piece of his sternum pushed through his chest."

"Darvis and Darrell."

"Darrell Ford," he said.

"He was a prick. I gave him a chance."

"Like the chance you gave Savage?"

"I gave Savage a chance. It's not my fault he still thought I was the victim when he decided."

"It *is* literally your fault he still thought you were the victim."

"Maybe. I really didn't want him to walk away."

"That was obvious as you dragged him around by the broken leg."

"He was trying to walk away after passing on the chance I offered."

"I'm not sure that was a walk."

I shrugged. "I don't feel better after it, but I do feel he got some of what he deserved."

"I looked up DeMarco. It was never made public what Savage did to that girl but there are records. No record is safe if I search for it. I understand what you did a lot better after seeing it. He deserved worse."

"He needed it ten years ago. I just wish I could have done it then."

"He would have torn you into little pieces ten years ago."

"True enough. Halleck came close and Savage was on a whole different level."

"Was?"

"Some of those bones will never heal back right even if they find a strength specialist to reset them. He'll feel them for the rest of his life. I don't pity him though. He needs to feel it every day."

"I looked into Ford a little and stopped fairly quickly," he said. "That fucker was as twisted as they come. The things he did to people in 'the Box' were *cringey*."

"I don't think that's a word."

"If you saw what I did you'd know it's a word."

"I saw what he was planning when the room started growing torture devices. I'll let it slide."

He looked around us at the buildings. "What exactly are you doing in Portland?"

"Thought I might visit some friends and set things straight."

"I thought as much when the phone pinged its location. No dust when you shift, now?"

"Nope. I've tested it a few times to be sure."

"I guess they need to be dealt with. Do you want me to handle techno boy?"

"No, I got it handled."

"I'll be looking for the fireworks in case you need backup."

I nodded. "Here's where I drop out of sight. Did you know there were a bunch of old tunnels under the city?"

I saw his eyes flash.

"Shanghai tunnels."

"That's just weird," I said. "It used to take you a minute."

"The new abilities are nice. I get to travel dressed."

"Yeah, if you can call it that," I said looking at the white coat with a fur collar. "At least you fit in with the people here."

He grinned. "Be careful. Everything I've seen from this bunch looks dangerous."

"I'll be careful, mom."

He sighed. "Whatever, you old reprobate."

I laughed and pulled a grate from the sidewalk open to drop down the hole.

# Chapter 44

"What good are you?" Kahn paced around the room in a big circle. "Where is he?"

"I told you he has someone very talented covering his digital footprint."

Milo stopped pacing and glared at Kane. "Technomancer." The word was spat out in distaste.

"You didn't seem to mind when I found what your pet flesh sculptor was doing in his off time."

"Peter Yarborough was a genius," Virginia said.

I laughed.

Virginia turned to look at the other people at the table. "Which one of you—"

She jumped out of her throne and sideways.

"What is the matter with you?" Milo asked. His voice dripped with disdain.

"My chair just pinched my ass!"

I projected my head from the back of the seat. "It's a lovely ass, Miss Madsen. I'm sorry I didn't get to see you last time I was here."

"You!"

I turned my head toward Khan. "Hi, Milo! How are ya?"

His eyes began to glow.

"Now, I wouldn't do that—"

The room was filled with a blinding flash as lightning impacted against me. There were short screams that cut off pretty quickly as the current flowed through my metal body which was connected to the backsides of three of the Elementals. Virginia had staggered backward and avoided the fate of the other three along the left side of the table.

Douglas Gant, Walter Kane, and a lovely lady sitting on the green throne didn't fare so well.

"Now Milo," I said, repairing some of the melted metal of my form. "Look what you've done to your friends."

I shifted, drawing in the mass that I had absorbed when I took the place of the four thrones. Three bodies dropped to the floor. I was facing Geneva Reyez whose body was beginning to glow.

I shook a finger. "Don't do it."

She released an intense burst of flame.

"None of you ever listen," I said and projected a pencil-thin rod of titanium across the space between us and through her right eye. "Unreasonable people make life so difficult."

I turned back just in time for Khan to hit me with another lightning bolt which carried down the rod still connected to Reyez who had stumbled into the fellow rising from the white throne who took a lot of the charge right into his shoulder. The metal throne under him took the current so it traveled down the arm to where his hand still rested on the arm of the chair.

"Milo!" Virginia screamed at the enraged Electromancer. "Stop!"

He turned to her.

I watched the guy I didn't know tumble to the floor, his right arm a blackened ruin.

I detected the pheromones she was putting off.

Milo didn't have his senses blocked from the pheromone and he staggered as they entered his system.

"That's a lovely smell," I said. "Lavender and rose?"

"They don't affect you, do they?"

"Just a pleasant scent," I said.

"Are you going to kill me?"

"Wasn't planning on it. Wasn't planning on killing anyone. I came to make something clear. I never took your money, nor did I agree to do the job. If you keep sending people after me, I'm going to get offended. I tried to explain to his brother. He did pretty much the same as this one and attacked. Now I'm tired of these pricks coming after me and I suggest that it ends. Make sure he understands that when he comes out of whatever that is."

I pointed to Milo who was swaying where he was standing.

"He'll never stop."

"That's his own funeral," I said. "Now my message is delivered, remember it. Come after me again and I will take everything from you."

I could see the hate in her eyes as she nodded.

I walked out of the *'council'* room.

"I'm craving some barbecue," I muttered as I walked out the front door of the Elemental Club.

I noticed a distinct lack of personnel working in the club. "They hit the bricks pretty fast."

I halted mid-stride as I watched my brother roll up in front of the club in his Bel Air. It took me a moment to realize it was my son. He reached across and pushed open the passenger door.

"Need a lift?"

I slid into the passenger seat.

"I talked to mom, and I realize it isn't your fault you were gone all those years. You never even knew. Thought I would do you a solid since I left you hanging in Georgia. Found this in a CIA site over in Roswell, New Mexico. You'd be surprised what all they have in that place."

I chuckled. "Thanks, son."

Annoyed with Lloyd

# Epilogue

The large house was back in the hills and had a wonderful view of the mountains. I stopped the car in the circle drive and opened the door. I thought the whole metal skin was cool, so I used it in my latest shift.

A shadow crossed the space from the house, and I looked up to see her drop and settle to the ground. She wore a loose-fitting tank top that barely covered anything and a pair of form-fitting pants. On her side was strapped a pistol that looked like a Colt 1911 to me.

"My twilight angel," I said. "Does the offer still stand?"

She smiled as she recognized the name. "I thought I would never see you again. And yes, the offer stands."

I motioned toward the car. "You ever ridden in a '55 Bel Air?"

"I haven't."

"Care to go for a spin?"

She smiled widely and jumped into my arms. "Maybe in a little while."

# Author Bio

Christopher Woods, writer of fiction, teller of tales, and professional liar was born way too long ago to be talking about and has spent most of his life with a book in hand. He is known for his popular Soulguard series and creating the shared universe in The Fallen World series. He has also written several short stories and the Legend series in the Four Horsemen Universe as well as some works in the Salvage Title Universe. With books ranging from fantasy to post-apocalyptic science fiction and military science fiction. There should be something for everyone. He lives in Woodbury, TN with his wife, Wendy. As a former carpenter of 25 years, he spends his time between various building projects and writing new books. To contact him go to https://www.theprofessionalliar.com and send him a message or find him on Facebook at https://www.facebook.com/chris.woods.37.

# Books by Christopher Woods

### <u>Soulguard series</u>
*Soulguard*

*Soullord*

*Bloodlord*

*Rash'Tor'Ri*

*Freedom's Prophet*

### <u>The Fallen World series</u>
*This Fallen World*

*Farmer's Creed*

*The Island of Doctor Laroue (w/Chris Kennedy)*

*Kade*

### <u>Four Horsemen Universe</u>
*Legend*

*Daskada, the Legend*

### <u>Anthologies including stories by Christopher Woods</u>
*Fistful of Credits*

*Luck is not a Factor*
*We Dare*
*The Dogs of God*
*Salvage Conquest*
*When Valor Must Hold*
*Through the Gate*
*We Dare: Semper Paratus*
*We Dare: Wanted, Dead or Alive*
*It Came From the Trailer Park*
*It Came From the Trailer Park 2*
*It Takes all Kinds*
*Starflight: Tales From the Starport Lounge*

## <u>Anthologies Edited by Christopher Woods</u>

*From the Ashes* (with Chris Kennedy)
Among the Embers (with Chris Kennedy)
*Give Me LibertyCon* (with Toni Weisskopf)
Onward, LibertyCon! (with Toni Weisskopf)

Annoyed with Lloyd.

We hope that you enjoyed this title and look forward to many more to come. Please, leave us a review! Reviews matter to all of our authors.

And don't forget to check out the latest edition of **Car Wars**

http://www.sjgames.com/car-wars/

Or the other amazing titles from Steve Jackson Games

http://www.sjgames.com

…or the latest in the Car Warriors: Autoduel Chronicle fiction series.
https://threeravenspublishing.com/car-warriors-autoduel-chronicles/

Take a look at some of our other award-winning series at
https://threeravenspublishing.com/series-universes/

Visit us at
https://www.threeravenspublishing.com and sign up for our newsletter for the latest and greatest news on upcoming titles and events.

Other series and titles you might enjoy.

ROBERT SILVERBERG
HAWKSBILL
TIMES TWO

The Dragon Award Nominated Series
FREE on Kindle Unlimited!

JOINT TASK FORCE 13
HOLDING THE LINE
BETWEEN HEAVEN AND HELL
AVAILABLE ON
AMAZON

MYSTERY,
MAGIC &
MAYHEM
WITH A TWIST
OF ROMANCE
J.F. POSTHUMUS
ON AMAZON
FIND ME

B.E.N.T.
BIOLOGIC    ENHANCED    NASCENT    TALENT

THE RAVEN
AND
THE CROW
MICHAEL K. FALCIANI
FIND ME
ON AMAZON

STARFLIGHT

IT CAME FROM THE
TRAILER PARK

You can also keep up to date with our latest release announcements on <u>Scifi.radio</u> and get some of the best fandom programing on the planet.

## Scifi for your Wifi

And don't forget to check out our other Sponsors and Affiliates

A southern Appalachian jewel for craft beer lovers, Buck Bald Brewing offers something for everyone. With delicious, locally brewed beverages from across the spectrum, Buck Bald Brewing offers craft brews that are consistently amazing.

From the dark and smooth Shesquatch Scottish ale, to the intense hops of

Hippibilly IPA, to the puckering sour of the blackberry and cinnamon in Berry My Heart at the Trailer Park, and more than 60+ rotating brews, you'll find what you're looking for and more.

With smiling faces behind the bar ready to help you find your next favorite brew, a constantly rotating selection of delicious craft beverages, toe-tapping tunes always playing, and the biggest games on TV, you can kick your feet up in either Copperhill, Tennessee or Murphy, North Carolina and immerse yourself in the Buck Bald Brewing experience. So, come out, fill a pint, fill a growler, and fill your mind at your new favorite family-owned craft brewery.

To discover more visit us at buckbaldbrewing.com or follow us on Facebook @buckbaldbrewing and @buckbaldbrewingmurphy.

Vesper Wren's
TRAILER PARK
PIXIE
PUNCH
· A PEACH STRAWBERRY SELTZER ·
BUCK BALD BREWING

BRAXTON
HICKS
MIDNIGHT MOCHA MILK
STOUT
BUCK BALD BREWING

Annoyed with Lloyd